Cat Tails
and
Spooky Trails

Mattie Meets
Bogey The Plantation Cat

Jean Hunt

Illustrated by Caroline Lott

To order additional copies of this book, please visit our website at www.jeanhuntcattales.com.

Profits from the sale of this book will be donated to organizations that benefit animals and wildlife.

Dedication

This book is dedicated
to my mother,
who taught me the joy
of loving animals

and

To my husband,
who continues to show
love and patience
with me, my strays, and my pets

and

To a very special girl
who always wanted
to hear Bogey's adventures

and

To all the wonderful people
who have loved and cared for Bogey
when we were away
from the cottage.

Blessed With Tenderness

Dear Father, hear and bless
Thy beasts and singing birds
And guard with tenderness
Small things that have no words.

–Author Unknown

One

A loud "clonk, clonk!" stomped across my porch. The sun glowed warm on my face and the birds sang as I napped on my favorite wicker sofa. *What was that loud bumping noise?* Slowly I opened one eye and peeked down at a pair of red cowboy boots. I yawned and forced the other eye open. The morning sun was so bright, I had to squint. Sunlight sparkled around her blond curls like a halo. Was she an angel? She had a huge frown on her face. Do angels frown? Nope, don't think so. I moved my head in the shade of the pillows to get a better view.

A spunky lookin' girl stood in front of me with her hands on her hips. Her jeans had holes in both knees and hung over the tops of her boots. Her white tee shirt had a dog's face on it. That should have been a clue. The toe of her cowboy boot tapped loudly on the wooden porch and scared the birds from the feeders. She cocked her head and glared at me. I glared right back.

Why was "Miss Red Boots" frowning? Most people smile at me. I guess my plans for a nap were ruined. But I REALLY had no idea what was gonna happen that day and the trouble she'd cause me.

I am a cat. My name is Bogey. I live on a plantation near the Waccamaw River in South Carolina and have a peaceful home. At least it was until the morning Mattie stomped across my porch and into my life. If I had known what my day was going to be like, I'd have put my paws over my eyes, flipped over and gone back to sleep. By late afternoon, I knew my life would never be the same. Some people say cats have nine lives. I might need more 'cause I used them all up the day I met her.

Two

My name is Mattie. I have a story to tell about a very special cat. But the problem is my dog. He doesn't like cats. And you know, if a dog is your best friend, you're not gonna tell him you're writing a story about a cat. I don't do cats either. At least I didn't until that day I found myself with a big, black and white fluffy cat named Bogey.

It all started on a cool morning. I woke up, snuggled down deep in my bed and planned my day. Water sprinkled across my face. I looked over at Gus in his fishbowl beside my bed. He jumped and splashed more water on me. I wiped my face with the top of my sheet.

Goldfish came from China. Light from the sun increases the gold color on the fish scales. Some goldfish can live 70 years.

His orange body sparkled as he swam in circles.

"You forgot, Gus. It's Saturday. We have the whole day together."

Gus blew a bubble and it popped. He does that when he gets excited.

The wind blew and a branch tapped gently on my bedroom window. I could have opened the window and climbed down my favorite tree. I've done this secretly many times, but I wasn't in the mood today.

Buddy, my hamster moved around in his cage at the foot of my bed.

"Good morning Buddy," I said and jumped out of bed. I ran to the window and pulled the curtains back to see if Tucker, my dog was awake. He's a labrador and my very best friend. He was half in and half out of his doghouse. *Was he outgrowing his doghouse already?* His head rested on his folded paws. He must be sound asleep.

Hamsters have pouches on both sides of their head, which they stuff full of food to be eaten later. Hamsters make entertaining household pets.

Muffy, the cat next door perched on the back wall. She swished her tail and glared at Tucker. Muffy and Tucker have never been friends.

My blue jeans with a hole in each knee lay crumpled up in the corner. I slipped them on quickly and grabbed my favorite tee shirt with a picture of Tucker on it. I took two tennis balls out of my red cowboy boots and put one in each pocket of my jeans. I pulled on my boots.

4

"Be back in a little while," I whispered to Gus and Buddy. I wanted to get outside and play with Tucker before Mom and Dad woke up. I tiptoed down the stairs so I wouldn't wake them.

Uh, oh. . .

Mom stood at the bottom of the steps.

"Good morning Mattie," smiled Mom.

"Oh. . . hi Mom," I stammered.

"Your Grandmomma, Nana, just called and invited you to spend the night at her new house. She bought a cottage that's on an old plantation."

"What's a plantation?" I asked.

"It's a farm where cotton and rice used to grow. Years ago in the South, big farms were called plantations."

"Well, what would I do on an old plantation?"

"You'll have fun with Nana. She's adopted a cat she found in the woods. She wants you to meet him."

"I don't actually like cats much. And I hate to leave Tucker. Can he go with me?"

"Maybe another time, but for your first visit, let's not upset Nana's cat. He may not like dogs."

"Well Tucker doesn't like cats either."

"You'd better ask Nana about bringing Tucker to meet her cat," Mom said.

"Is he a wild cat like the one at the zoo?"

"No. Not really, but he did live in the woods before Nana found him."

"Why does she want a cat anyway?" I asked.

"Because she loves animals like you do," said Mom.

"Aw, Mom. I already have big plans today."

"You do?" asked Mom.

"Tucker and I are going to play ball and have fun." I said.

"I'm sure Nana has a fun day planned for you."

"Oh, Mom. This cat probably purrs instead of barks," I groaned. "And he won't wanna play with me."

"With all the woods around Nana's cottage, you'll have fun pretending and exploring. I know you like to do that."

"Not unless there's some wildlife in the woods." I wrinkled up my nose. "Am I gonna have to pretend this cat's a tiger? Is the cat the only animal that lives on the plantation?"

Mom cocked her head and grinned, "I don't know, Mattie. I guess you'll just have to find out."

"Mom. . . do you know something you're not telling me?"

"Hmm," said Mom with a smile.

I stared at Mom and patted my toe.

"I NEVER get to do what I want."

"Mattie, PLEASE quit whining," said Mom.

"But, Mom. I don't know anything about cats. What would I do with a cat all day? Sounds boring," I said.

I dragged myself back up the stairs stomping my boot on each step. I tripped a little and almost fell.

I finally made it to my room and snatched my overnight bag out of the closet.

Mom walked in and said, "I'll help you pack. Do you want to take your new stuffed cat?"

"Oh, I don't care. I just use it for a pillow."

"Nana would probably like to see it since she has a cat now."

"Okay, I guess I'll take it." I pouted.

Mom frowned at me.

"See you downstairs, young lady," she said.

"Sorry Gus and Buddy. I can't take you outside today. Mom called off our play day," I sighed.

Buddy hung on the bars of his cage and looked at me with a sad face. Gus slapped the water with his tail.

I snatched the cat pillow off my bed and crammed it in my bag. I yanked the zipper to close the bag. The cat's whiskers got caught in the zipper. I tugged backwards on the zipper to get the whiskers out, but it wouldn't budge.

"Come on, Mattie! You're taking too long!" Mom called out.

"Yes, Ma'am, I'm coming!" I huffed.

I quickly picked up Buddy's cage, stumbled over the rug and banged the cage against the bed. He rolled over and bumped his head.

"I'm so sorry Buddy," I said.

I placed Buddy's cage next to Gus' fish bowl so they could be together for the day.

"See you two tomorrow," I said. "Tucker will come up to check on you later."

Mom must have let Tucker inside. He heard his name and bounced up the stairs. He stared at my overnight bag. He knew I was leaving.

I looked at his sad eyes. His tail was tucked between his legs.

"Tucker, are you okay?" I asked.

He cocked his head and whined.

The Labrador Retreiver is the most popular breed of dog in the world and was first found in Newfoundland, Canada. They are good-natured dogs and make loveable pets for children.

"Don't cry, Tucker. You're a big Labrador," I said.

I leaned down and gave him a kiss on top of his head. His tail wagged now.

"Be nice to Gus and Buddy, Tucker. Sometime when I go to Nana's you can go with me, *if* Tucker and I mean *if,* you can learn to like cats. Work on that while I'm gone, will ya? Start practicing on Muffy. Don't pick any fights."

Tucker cocked his head again and looked puzzled.

"Tucker, you know exactly what I'm talking about." I spelled it out for him. "C . . . A . . . T . . . S!"

8

Three

We drove along in silence for a while. I slumped down in my seat and crossed my arms. I couldn't think of a thing to say. My day was ruined.

"We're here, Mattie," said Mom as she parked the car under a huge tree. Something that looked like dirty hair hung down from the tree and brushed across the windshield.

"That tree looks like a giant with a messy beard!"

The name "live oak" comes from the fact that these oaks remain green during winter. The famous tree named "Angel Oak" on John's Island, South Carolina is 1400 years old. The branches of a live oak can reach 70 feet in length.

"They're called live oaks, Mattie and that's Spanish moss hanging from the limbs."

"It'd make a great wig when I play dress up."

"Don't do that Mattie. Bugs live in the moss."

"I don't care!"

Mom glared over at me.

"Wow! Nana's cottage is really in the woods," I said. "What's that over there? It looks like a lake. Great! I can go swimming."

"No you can't. It's a marsh and it can be deep at high tide. Don't go too close, Mattie. You might fall in," warned Mom.

"Come on, Mom," I huffed. "That's silly. You know I can swim."

"Mattie, you wouldn't want to swim in the marsh."

"Well, why not?"

Mom didn't have time to answer because I heard something.

"Is that the ocean? Where is it? Is it close by? Do you think Nana plans for us to go there? I could swim and ride the waves."

"The ocean's over there," Mom said and pointed, "But it's a little cool to be on the beach today."

"Oh, but I want to go today," I whined. "I can collect shells if I can't go in the water. Nana might let us go if I asked her. I bet if I climbed one of those tall trees over there, I could see the ocean."

"Mattie, don't get hurt on the first day you're here," said Mom.

"But I like to climb trees. If I can't go to the ocean, I could at least see it."

"Mattie, please quit fussin' and get out of the car," said Mom.

I tugged my bag out of the back seat.

"What's sticking out of your bag Mattie?" Mom asked.

"Oh, nothin'. Just stuff," I stammered.

"Looks like whiskers to me," Mom said with a frown.

A door slammed. I looked towards the cottage. Nana stood on the front porch dusting her hands on her apron.

"Nana," I shouted as I ran to the porch, excited now to see her.

I dashed up the steps and wrapped my arms around Nana. She kissed me on my cheek. I looked up at Nana and grinned.

"I see the tooth fairy visited you, Mattie," said Nana.

"Yes ma'am, she took my tooth and left me money under my pillow. I'm saving it to buy Tucker a new tennis ball."

Mom and Nana hugged and talked about Nana's cottage.

I looked around at the giant trees.

"Wow, these trees must be a hundred years old Nana!" I said.

"Yes, I'm sure they are, Mattie. The plantation used to reach from the river and rice fields way over there..." she pointed, "all the way to the ocean. This house was once a hunting lodge..."

I didn't let Nana finish because I got a whiff of cookies and said, "You smell just like cookies."

"Well, I guess I do. I've been baking your favorite... chocolate chip."

"Are they ready?"

"Not quite, but they will be shortly."

Mom turned to me and said, "Mattie, you be sweet and have a great time. I'll pick you up tomorrow."

Mom gave me a big hug and walked down the steps. Nana and I waved as Mom drove the car out of the driveway.

"Mattie, what is that sticking out of your bag?" asked Nana.

"Oh, just whiskers," I said.

"Well, speaking of whiskers, I want you to meet my new cat," said Nana. "Look at *his* long white whiskers. Isn't his black and white fur beautiful? It's so thick and his nose is the pinkest I've ever seen. Don't you agree, Mattie?"

I didn't have a good answer for that.

"Well...I guess so," I managed to say.

"I named him BOGEY," said Nana proudly.

I put my bag down and walked over to the wicker sofa. It was full of fluffy pillows. There in the middle sat the fattest cat I had ever seen. His eyes glared at me and I glared right back.

I thought to myself, *is this day going to be all about Bogey?*

"Do you have a dog too, Nana? I love to play with dogs."

"No, Mattie. I don't have a dog. But you can pick up Bogey and pet him if you'd like to."

"That's okay, Nana. I don't want to." *That was the last thing I wanted to do. I didn't even know how to pick up a cat.*

"Bogey has lots to show you here on the plantation. I'm sure you'll have a good time looking around. Uh oh, I smell my cookies. They're in the oven." She dashed inside the house. "Don't go too close to the marsh," Nana yelled over her shoulder.

That made me wonder why. Mom said it might be deep, or was there something in there they didn't want me to see? What was it? Giant fish, monsters, dragons or what? I would just have to take a tiny peep, wouldn't I?

Alone on the front porch, I put my hands on my hips, huffed and tapped my toe. I stared at the cat. He stared right back.

"It's rude to stare at people," I said.

In one quick motion, that cat jumped off the porch. He pranced down an old brick path with his bushy tail high in the air.

He didn't even look back at me. Tucker would have licked my hand, wagged his tail, barked or something.

"Wow, that cat's got a real attitude," I snickered and shrugged my shoulders.

He stopped, turned and looked at me.

"So... what are you looking at? Silly cat!" I said.

I stayed on the porch and stood on my tiptoes looking for the marsh I wasn't supposed to go near. I wondered why nobody wanted me close to the marsh. *I'd just have to find out, wouldn't I?*

But that cat caught my eye. It's hard to miss a cat that big. He yawned, arched his back up and stretched his legs.

"Are you coming slow-poke?" said a little voice.

"Who said that?" I asked.

I looked around. I didn't see anybody.

"Who's calling me slow-poke?"

No one was there except that cat.

Four

That cat walked away from me down the path. He stopped, turned his head back and stared at me.

"Well, are you coming?" a little voice said.

I looked around the porch and out into the garden. No one was there. I listened. All was quiet.

Is my pretending getting out of control? I'm now hearing voices.

I felt a little silly answering, but huffed "Well . . .I'll just poke around until you decide to come out of hiding. I can play games too."

I walked over towards the watery marsh. That cat followed me. I strained my neck to see better, but still couldn't get a good view of the marsh. I looked down at the cat sitting there by a huge tree.

"Well, Cat you can sit right here, but I'm curious about who's talking to me. They could be near the water. Do you know? Of course you don't. You're just a cat. I'll have a look at the marsh. You stay here by yourself, Cat. Purr, catch mice or whatever it is you do. I'll go have a peek for myself."

I strolled across the grass towards the marsh.

"Whoa... don't go near the marsh!" There was that little voice speaking again, this time louder.

"Who said that?" I hollered.

I sprinted back across the yard and looked behind the big tree. No one was there.

"Okay, come on out. I'm not in the mood for hide and seek today. I only play that with my dog, Tucker," I yelled.

"I'm not hiding. I'm standing right beside you," said the voice.

Startled, I looked down. There was only that silly cat sitting by my red boots.

"Are you talking... to me?" I asked loudly.

I waited. Silence.

"No, no. I'm still pretending, that's it," I mumbled.

"Nope, you're not pretending. Animals talk. You just have to learn to listen," he said clearly.

I stooped down and put my face inches from his face.

"Are you kidding me, Cat?" I asked.

"No," a quiet answer came out of nowhere.

"Okay, I'm listening, Cat. Say something. I want to see if your mouth moves. Talk to me Cat... IF... you can."

"If we're going to talk, quit shouting and stop calling me 'Cat'." His mouth moved as he spoke.

16

My heart pounded wildly against my chest. I sat down with a thump and leaned my head back against the tree. I closed my eyes a second. *Maybe I was dreaming.* I slowly opened my eyes. Nope…he's still there.

I held my head in my hands.

"OH . . . , HE'S REALLY TALKING!" I said.

I can't believe it!

Finally, I looked up. His mouth still moved as he spoke.

"My real name is Bogey. What's your real name?"

I stood up, threw my shoulders back, tried to act calm and said, "My real name is Marian Elizabeth Hannah, but you can call me Mattie. If I'm not pretending and you're really talking to me, tell me some things I want to know, like what's in the marsh? Prove to me that you're speaking… BOGEY."

"Lots of things are in the marsh. Mainly fish and…"

"There has to be something else, like big creatures. I wanna see them for myself," I shouted.

"Do you always talk so much and so loud? You're enough to scare the fish, and the birds are spooked by your shouting."

"What…?" I yelled.

"Shh! Will you hush? Look up at the sky," said Bogey.

We both looked up over the water and saw big birds flying and chattering. They looked like little airplanes to me.

"Is that a fish in one of their beaks?" I asked Bogey.

"Yep. They eat frogs too. They're called Blue Herons," he said.

"Yuck! That's totally disgusting! Those poor frogs!"

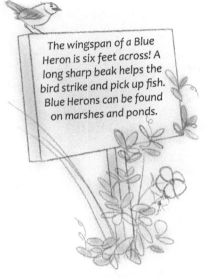

The wingspan of a Blue Heron is six feet across! A long sharp beak helps the bird strike and pick up fish. Blue Herons can be found on marshes and ponds.

"It's their food," he said.

I had eased closer to the marsh. Maybe there were giant frogs in the water. I started to ask Bogey when the tall grass near the edge of the marsh rustled and swayed back and forth. I turned my head and looked at Bogey.

Bogey froze.

"What is it?" I whispered.

His ears flattened back and he squatted close to the ground. He looked afraid. I watched the rippling grass to see what had him so nervous. We heard a huge splash!

"Quick! Run!" yelled Bogey. "He's coming out and he's huge!"

"What? Who's coming out?" I screamed.

"Run! He's headed straight for us," Bogey shouted.

Five

"**R**un Mattie, run! The alligator's climbing out of the marsh!" Bogey yelled.

It took a second for my legs to move. I glanced back at the marsh. My eyes opened wide. I ran.

The alligator dragged his long tail up on dry land. He moved fast in our direction.

"He's right behind us. Help, Bogey!" I screamed.

I'd only seen pictures of alligators. A live one is even scarier, especially if he's chasing you!

Bogey shouted, "Run for the woods, Mattie! Zigzag! Run left and then right!" Bogey glanced over his shoulder as he ran.

I ran ahead of Bogey in a crisscross pattern. Branches pricked my hands and face as I pushed them out of my way. I looked back over my shoulder and Bogey was behind me. He was zigzagging through the trees.

"Is he gaining on us, Bogey?" I shouted.

No answer.

I drew my breath in sharply and ran as fast as I could.

I've heard alligators eat cats. Would he eat Bogey and take a bite out of me? Or eat all of me?

As soon as I dared, I looked back again. The alligator's big feet slowed down. He made a wide circle dragging his heavy tail and turned back towards the marsh.

"We're safe Bogey!" I shouted, "We're safe! He's going away. Whew! Glad that's over. Why did we zigzag? That was hard to do in the woods with all the trees!" I yelled.

Bogey caught up with me and panted, "Alligators can't zigzag."

We looked at each other.

He looked scary with his mouth open and his sharp teeth showing. I stepped backwards and took a deep breath.

"You look like a bob cat panting like that," I said.

"Well, you look like a chipmunk with nuts in your cheeks."

I guess I'd been holding my breath.

"Let your breath out, Mattie."

"Whew!" I took a huge gulp of fresh air and felt better.

"Wow! That was close. He must have been ten feet long. Now I know why Nana said for us to stay away from the marsh."

I looked at Bogey. He was walking away. Was he leaving me here?

"Hey! Wait for me, Bogey!" I sputtered. "Where are you going? That alligator may turn back around."

I looked over my shoulder and walked fast until I was beside Bogey.

Bogey's whiskers moved up and down and his ears laid back. His big bushy tail swished back and forth. His pink nose glowed as bright as Rudolph's.

"Hey, what's wrong? Where are you going? " I asked as he walked off. "Wait a minute!"

I plopped down on the ground and pulled my socks up tighter in my boots.

Bogey came back and sat beside me.

"You went too close to the water," Bogey said with a frown. "I had to tempt the alligator to chase me. Alone, I could have climbed a tree and been safe. But I had to look after Miss Nosey. You're really too curious for me. That alligator could have had me for supper and you for dessert."

"Oh, don't talk like that, Bogey."

I hate it when people get mad at me.

I began to twist a curl around my finger.

"I only wanted a peek at the marsh," I tried to explain, "I didn't know what *really* was in there. Don't be so grumpy. We got away, didn't we?" I asked, my voice a little shaky.

Alligators feed on fish, turtles, birds and frogs and have webbed feet. Some alligators can be dangerous to humans.

21

Bogey stared me straight in the eye and said, "You don't know how close that was, Mattie." His big tail swished. "You're from in town. You don't know much about the wildlife here. So, could you just listen next time, okay?"

I shrugged and said, "Maybe."

Bogey rolled his eyes, frowned and his tail shot straight up in the air. He turned his back to me and marched away. What a strut that cat had!

"Wait Bogey!" I screamed.

I jumped up and ran to catch him. He walked faster and I talked faster.

"Listen, I know a lot about wildlife. I went to the zoo once. I've seen tigers, monkeys and gorillas. I've even petted a big elephant. Don't think you know everything about the animals. I know a lot too."

He stopped and I caught up with him.

"Yeah, but the animals you saw were all in cages," Bogey said as he narrowed his eyes at me. "The animals here are all in the wild. You need to learn to respect the place they call their home."

His little mouth was really moving now.

I couldn't believe that bossy cat was giving me a speech. It sounded a little like the lecture my dad gave me last week.

Bogey seemed serious. I twisted my hair around my fingers, looked down at him and listened for a few minutes. I couldn't take my eyes off his face. His nose had a big scratch like an old scar. There was a nip out of one of his ears. For this cat to be only a foot tall, he gave a BIG lecture.

In a huff, I flung my arms out. *Will he ever hush?*

I stared down at my hands.

"What's wrong with your hands?" Bogey asked.

"Oh, nothin. Just scratched, nicked, cut up and bloody, that's all," I said.

"How did that happen?"

"I don't know. Guess grabbing branches as I ran from that alligator. Maybe I could wash them somewhere?"

"You can rinse your hands in our new birdbath," Bogey said and pointed his paw in the direction of a path lined with giant trees.

I hurried down the path and looked up. I saw something on a limb that stopped me in my tracks. Bogey almost bumped into the back of me but walked between my boots.

I stooped down and put my hand on his back to stop him. I whispered, "What is that? It looks like a fox."

Bogey looked up and said, "That's because it is. It's a Gray Fox."

"I saw a red fox one time, but it wasn't in a tree. How'd he get up there?"

"He climbed. The Gray Fox climbs trees. You didn't know that?"

I threw my hands down by my sides and huffed, "Bogey, you think you know everything."

"Maybe I do," said Bogey and rolled his eyes at me. "Come on. The birdbath is over there."

I gave the ground a swift kick with my boot and followed Bogey with my head down. I kept silent. *Silly Cat, thinks he smarter than me.* I puckered my lips and marched on.

A little smaller than the Red Fox, the Gray Fox is the only member of the dog family known to climb trees.

"Mattie, watch where you're going!" said Bogey "You almost ran into that tree."

I stopped just in time and looked up at the giant trunk in front of me. I walked around the other side of the tree and spotted the birdbath.

"Wow, that really is a big birdbath," I said and ran over to it.

"When I first saw it," Bogey said, "I thought it was my new food bowl. I got real excited. Then I found out it was a birdbath."

"I'd already guessed you like to eat, but a birdbath full of food would've been too much, even for you."

Bogey jumped up on the edge of the birdbath and lapped a few sips of water.

I rinsed off my dirty hands in the cool water and patted them dry on my jeans.

A tall tree stood beside the birdbath.

"Look, that's a great tree to climb, Bogey!" I said. "I bet I can see the ocean from the top."

"Yep, you'd see the ocean all right. But I climb the tree to watch the birds bathe. They're funny splashing around and ducking their heads under the water. We can sit here under the tree and watch them if you want to."

I was half way up the tree before Bogey could say another word. The limbs worked like a ladder. I climbed almost to the top.

"Wait a minute!" He screamed out. "That's far enough. You're going to fall!"

"I know how to climb trees, Bogey," I called down to him.

Bogey leaped off the birdbath, landing on the limb just below me. It was a pretty good leap considering his size.

"Wow, Bogey. You can really jump high!" I cheered. "You could be in the circus. I'm going to move around the tree so I can get a better view. Scoot over, will you? I need to put my foot on your branch…" I shifted my weight onto the limb where Bogey sat.

"Mattie! This isn't going to be good! Let's go down before you…"

I put my arms around the tree trunk and put all my weight on Bogey's limb.

The limb made a crackling noise and snapped off from the tree. Bogey reached up to grab the branch above him. He missed. I hugged the tree trunk and watched as Bogey slipped and started to tumble down. I stretched out my hand to save him . . . .

Too late.

Six

Bogey fell through the air. He bounced against the tree trunk and hit branches all the way down.

"Bogey!" I cried out.

He landed in the birdbath with a big splash.

I scrambled down the tree and jumped from the bottom branch. My heart pounded against my tee shirt. I was really gonna be in trouble if I hurt Nana's cat.

I picked him up out of the birdbath. He was soaking wet and looked smaller.

"Are you okay, Bogey?"

"Not exactly," he said quietly. "I hate being wet and I think a limb scratched my nose."

I sat on the ground under the tree with Bogey. Water dripped from his fur and tail. His tail wasn't bushy anymore. It looked like a long black snake.

"Bogey, are you scared of snakes?"

"Yeah, why?"

"Cause that's what your tail looks like."

"It'll dry."

I pulled my tee shirt out of my jeans and rubbed his tail and fur with it. I softly patted his nose and blood smeared on my tee shirt.

"You're hurt," I said shocked.

I rubbed his fur again.

"I'll dry, Mattie. So please stop rubbing my fur backwards. Cats don't like that."

"Oh, I didn't know." I said. "Are you mad at me for making you fall?"

"No, not real mad. But I know now you're going to be more trouble than I'd first thought. Look at me. I'm a mess! For the rest of the day, will you please listen to me?"

"Ok, Bogey, can we forget about this? Let's go have some fun now."

"That'd be great, Mattie, 'cause so far, I'm *not* having fun."

Trying to change the subject, I said, "Let's go meet some animals that don't eat or bite you. Maybe we could go further in the woods. Don't you have any animal friends that live there?"

"Yeah, I do," Bogey said, "But you're going to have to be careful. It's sometimes dangerous out here. Like the other day, I got curious and peeked down a little hole near the marsh and a huge crab claw popped out and grabbed my nose! He wouldn't let go. I shook my head back and forth with him hanging on. I finally knocked him off with my paw. My nose was bloody for days. I didn't know that hole was his home. But I do now. My curiosity got me in trouble that time and yours almost got us both in trouble this time."

"I guess you're as curious as I am," I told Bogey.

"Yep, cats are curious, but I know these woods. I lived in them and you haven't. You're gonna have to listen to me. Don't let your curiosity and pretending get out of control again."

Cats have remarkable night vision, keen smell and hearing and can turn their ears to focus on different sounds. There are about 600 million house cats world-wide.

"Are you through lecturing?"

"No, not really," he said.

I puffed and blew away the curl hanging in my eye.

"Well, let's go play. Can we go see your friends, Bogey? Can we?"

"Randy, my friend, lives in the big tree by the carriage house," Bogey said.

"Can I meet him?" I asked.

"Yeah, if you want to," Bogey answered. "He's my best friend."

I followed Bogey into the woods where the big oak trees were thicker and the light grew dimmer. Vines hung down like long fingers trying to touch me.

"Which tree? I can't see anything." Moss drooped and tickled my nose. I pushed it away with my hand. "This is a real forest where elves and fairies and giants live," I whispered to myself. "Something could be hiding behind these big tree trunks and jump out and grab me. And I would be gone and you wouldn't know what happened because you can't see anything in here either."

"What are you talking about?" Bogey asked.

"Oh, nothing," I fibbed a little bit. "I just can't see where I'm going."

"Your eyes will get used to it being dimmer under the trees," said Bogey. "Cats can see in the dark. Trust me. There's nothing in here for you to be afraid of."

"Well, these giant trees could come alive and surround us and you can see better than me. You could squeeze between them and run and I would be left here with these green giants. And I'll bet there's lots of spider webs and creepy crawlies hiding on their limbs. They might get stuck all over my face and caught in my hair and a real big spider might crawl in my curls and live there all night and the creepy crawlies…"

"Mattie, will you hush? And quit twisting your hair! This was your idea to come into the forest. Do you want to meet Randy or are you ready to go home?"

"No, I want to see Randy. I just don't see him. I'll bet a big giant ate him."

"He's in one of these trees," Bogey replied. "The forest and trees are home to lots of animals, especially my friends, but no giants."

"I'd love to have a house in the trees! Would your friends mind if I climbed up to see their tree house? I'll take my boots off!"

I leaned on the tree and began to tug off my right boot.

"No, stop! You can't do that, Mattie. These oak trees are hard to climb. Especially for you 'cause you don't have claws. The limbs are too high for you to reach."

I reached out and grabbed a vine hanging down.

"I could put my feet on the tree and pull my way up on this vine like monkeys do."

Bogey shook his head "no" and shouted, "Randy, where are you?"

"Raaandy, where aaare yoooou?" It echoed back winding its way through the trunks of the trees.

"That sounds like an owl hooting. Are there owls in here? Will they bite me?"

Before Bogey answered, something hit me hard on the top of my head.

Seven

I crouched down, "Somebody's in that tree Bogey. They threw something at me." I whispered.

Bogey rolled his eyes.

I rubbed the top of my head. "Ouch! That hurt."

"Mattie, it was only a nut. Don't start whining again."

Bogey looked to the top of the tree.

"Randy, stop that!" he called. "She's a friend of mine."

"Randy likes to show off," Bogey whispered in my ear.

"Sorry Bogey. I was just having a little fun," said Randy. "She was groaning and moaning so much, I couldn't resist throwing a nut at her. Where'd you get such a creature? Did she throw you in the marsh, Bogey? I see you got yourself wet!"

"Where is he?" I asked. "Do all your friends talk?"

Bogey didn't answer, but pointed with his paw and I saw an animal a little bigger than Bogey. Actually, he was kind of pudgy like Bogey. They must eat together a lot. He had round, black eyes and looked like he had a black mask on. He scampered down to the ground.

"What kind of creature did you bring us, Bogey? She sure knows how to complain and whine," said Randy.

"This *creature*, as you call her is a little lady. Or at least her Nana thinks she's a little lady. I haven't seen that side of her yet."

"Hi, little lady, I'm Randy," he said.

"Hi Randy. My name's Mattie."

"Oh," I said. "You're a real live raccoon."

"I guess you could say that since I'm alive and I am a raccoon."

The name raccoon means "washing bear." Raccoons often dunk their food in water before they eat it. They also wash their hands after they have eaten.

"I saw a picture of a raccoon in my library book."

"I didn't know my picture was in a book," said Randy as he puffed up proudly.

"Maybe it wasn't you," Bogey said. "Could have been your cousin."

"Maybe," said Randy.

"Do you stay in fights a lot?" I asked. I leaned over and whispered to Bogey, "I had a black eye once when I got hit by a softball."

Bogey laughed and said, "This is what all raccoons look like."

"Well," Randy said, "We raccoons are known to put up a good fight, but I was born with these black eyes and my mask. Since we are discussing what *I* look like, what about you?"

"I don't have black eyes or a mask. What do you mean?" I asked.

"You have a tooth missing. Did *you* get in a fight?"

"No," I said proudly. "It fell out, and I put it under my pillow."

"What for?" said Bogey and Randy at the same time.

"The tooth fairy took my tooth, and left me some money."

"You *are teasing* us aren't you?" Randy snickered. "What would a fairy do with old teeth? And what is a fairy?"

I shrugged and said, "I have no idea what she does with the teeth, but fairies are beautiful, tiny creatures that fly and live in trees."

Randy scratched his head and stared at Bogey. He put his arm around him, leaned in and whispered, "Ya know that hole in my tree, Bogey?" asked Randy. "It's almost full of tiny teeth now. Do you think that's where that stash of teeth came from? The fairies?"

"Yep," Bogey said, "Guess that solves the teeth mystery."

I looked up and high in the tree was a large hole.

"Is that the hole with the moss hanging out of it?" I asked.

"Yeah," said Randy. "We take the moss out everyday and it's back in the hole the next morning. We can't figure it out."

"Maybe the fairies hide the teeth with the moss," I said.

"Will you two boost me up so I can look at the teeth? One of them might be mine," I said.

"That's not gonna work, Mattie," said Bogey. "Actually, you're too heavy for us."

I stared at the hole and said, "Maybe the fairies save the teeth for a while, then grind them up to use for fairy dust."

"Fairy dust?" asked Randy.

"It's dust that fairies use to sprinkle around to make magical things happen, like making flowers dance."

Randy shook his head and sighed, "Whatever . . . ."

"Randy, didn't you ever see a fairy fly in and drop teeth in the hole?" I asked.

Randy looked at Bogey, grinned and answered, "Nope! Didn't see one."

"If Randy had," Bogey added, "He probably would have eaten it. He eats anything."

"Oh, how awful to eat a fairy, Randy," I said.

"Bogey's teasing you, Mattie about me eating a tooth fairy. I probably would've gotten choked. Actually, we've never seen a fairy."

I shrugged and said, "Gee, what a shame!" I took a step backwards and looked at the limb where Randy had sat and asked, "So, what were you doing so high in that tree, looking at the ocean?"

"I can see the ocean from up there," Randy told me, "but I was actually napping. I like to sleep on a limb during the day. I come down at night to play with Bogey."

"At *night*? Aren't you two afraid of the dark! What about the things creeping around in the woods? They could bite or eat you."

Randy frowned, thumped his tail on the ground and said, "Those 'things', as you call them, are our friends… so of course we're not afraid."

Spanish moss began to fall from the tree. Most of it landed with a plop on my head. It stuck in my curls. I shielded my face with my hands. I peeked at Bogey and nothing fell on him.

I jumped out from underneath the branch and moved closer to Bogey.

Randy giggled, threw his head back and laughed out loud.

The stuff was all tangled in my curls. It hurt to pull it out. I stomped my foot.

"What's happening?" I whined.

Eight

"Wiggles, stop throwing stuff," Bogey called out.

"That's my squirrel friend," Bogey whispered to me.

"Come down, Wiggles and meet Mattie," Bogey shouted up through the tree limbs.

Wiggles scurried down the big tree headfirst and landed on the ground with a big plop.

He looked up at me, shrugged and grinned, "Whoops! Sorry it landed on your head. I was trying to clean out the hole in the tree. Someone puts moss in it everyday. I like to sit in that hole and look around and moss makes me itch. So I pitched it over my shoulder." His gray bushy tail wiggled when he talked.

"Mattie you kinda look good with gray hair, don't you think so, Bogey?" asked Wiggles.

Randy and Bogey giggled.

I hate it when somebody laughs at me.

I frowned at Wiggles. I yanked the nasty mess from my hair and threw it on the ground.

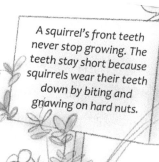

A squirrel's front teeth never stop growing. The teeth stay short because squirrels wear their teeth down by biting and gnawing on hard nuts.

Something gray slithered out from underneath the moss and darted away.

"Yuck!" I yelled and jumped away. Did you see that, Bogey? He must have been eight inches long!"

"What?" asked Bogey.

"Something crawled out of that moss . . . like . . . maybe a lizard?" I shivered and said.

"Probably was a lizard. Lots of insects and lizards live in the moss," Wiggles explained.

"But that was in my hair!" I moaned. I pointed with both hands to my head.

No one paid any attention to me. All three kept on talking about what they planned to eat for supper. No one looked at me. I bent over and shook my head. Stuff fell out. "You three might like lizards and insects hanging in your fur, but I don't. Is it all out?" I asked.

No one answered.

"It's not like there's a mirror out here," I said to myself.

I stomped my foot.

"Will someone please help me?"

They all turned and stared at me. Randy rolled his black eyes and said, "Don't you like lizards?"

"Who would like lizards?" I shouted.

Everyone stared at me with a puzzled look.

"Okay, so the lizard was kinda cute. He looked like a tiny alligator with that tail of his swishing around, but I wouldn't want him for a pet," I said.

"When I was hungry once, I ate a lizard's tail. Wasn't too bad," said Bogey.

"You did what?" I asked.

"I ate a lizard's tail," he said.

"Can't believe you," I said. "Poor lizard! Think what his mom thought when he came home without a tail."

"Lizard's tails grow back and his did," said Bogey.

"I ate one too," said Randy puffing up, "But I ate the whole lizard! It was pretty good!"

"How awful! Bet your breath smelled bad," I said.

Wiggles chuckled and said, "I chased one, but I like acorns better than lizards."

"Does anyone care that a lizard almost crawled through my hair?" I asked.

Bogey, Randy and Wiggles only stared at me like they couldn't think of a thing to say.

Suddenly their eyes widened. Bogey's and Randy's tails swished. Wiggles' little mouth dropped open and he quickly slapped his paws over it.

"Were you gonna say something, Wiggles?" I asked.

He shook his head back and forth with his paws clamped tightly over his mouth.

Bogey's eyes blinked. He raised his paw as if to touch me, but stopped in mid air. He started to say something, but all that came out was a tiny noise like a hiccup.

"What Bogey? What's wrong?" I asked. I looked at the three of them.

Silence.

Finally, Randy said, "Mattie, stoop down here by me."

"What? What's wrong?" I said as I squatted and leaned close to Randy.

He reached up and pulled at something in my hair.

"Ouch!" I said. "What are you doing?"

"WELL GEE! The thing keeps moving!" said Randy.

"WHAT'S MOVING?" I shouted. I tried to jerk away from Randy.

"Be still a minute, will ya?" Randy roared. "It's all tangled in your curls. It's almost out. There we go, Mattie. It's out."

"WHAT'S OUT? WHAT IS IT?" I screamed.

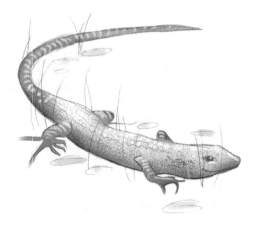

Nine

I rubbed my head where Randy had pulled my curls. Out of the corner of my eye, I saw something squirm in Randy's paw. I turned my head and stared.

"AHHHH!" I screamed.

"Does anybody want a lizard for supper?" Randy asked.

I scrambled to get out of the way and fell backwards. I ended up flat on my back. That's the last place I wanted to be with lizards crawling on the ground.

"Let him go! Let him go, Randy!" I shouted.

"Okay. If you say so, Mattie," said Randy.

Randy slowly eased the lizard to the ground, right next to my boot. He slithered towards me.

I scooted backwards on the ground like a crab.

"Not near me! He's creepy!" I screamed. "Pick it up! Pick it up! Quick!"

"Well, make up your mind, Mattie," said Randy.

Randy picked the lizard up again by the tail. He dangled the lizard over his open mouth. "Look quick before his tail comes off."

All of us stared at the squirming thing!

"Throw him in the bushes, quick!" I shouted. "Don't eat him, Randy!"

With a twinkle in his black eyes and a little smirk, Randy grinned and waddled towards me swinging the lizard. He pushed the wiggling monster in front of my face.

I screamed.

"He won't hurt you," Wiggles said.

I screamed louder.

"Stop, Randy. She's getting scared," Bogey finally said.

"Okay," Randy said. "I just wondered if she wanted to pet it."

"No! Get it away from me!" I shouted.

Randy slung the lizard in circles around his head winding up for a big throw. I got dizzy keeping my eyes on Randy's prize. Finally, Randy let go. Wiggles and Bogey ducked as the lizard sailed over their heads. They doubled over laughing.

"Great pitch, Randy," giggled Wiggles.

The little gray squirrel wiggled all over. He held on to his stomach. Now I know why they call him, Wiggles.

"That was cruel! And mean!" I said.

"No, it wasn't," said Wiggles. "How often does a lizard get a chance to fly? He landed on the soft moss and his tail didn't even come off."

"All of you think you are cute and funny. But do you know what could have happened?" I groaned. "If Randy hadn't pulled that lizard out of my curls, it would have ridden home in my hair. I wouldn't have felt a thing until I went to sleep. That yucky thing would have sneaked out of my hair and crept onto my pillow. He would have slithered over my face and tried to crawl in my . . . my. . . mouth!"

"Mmm. Yum. What a great snack!" Randy said.

I laid my arms across my chest and huffed.

"I, for one, am not a fan of lizard meat," I said with my nose turned up.

All three snickered at me. I raised one eyebrow and shook my head.

"I sure wish Lucky would have been here to see that lizard fly through the air," Wiggles said and grinned.

"He would have loved that!" said Bogey.

"He's so fast, his paw would've snatched that lizard out of the air before it hit the ground," said Randy clapping his hands and doubled over laughing.

If grabbed, the tail of some lizards separates from its body. The tail left behind wiggles to confuse the enemy!

"Who's Lucky?" I asked.

"Lucky is Wiggles' cousin. But Lucky's fur is black with a little white," said Bogey. "He's called a fox squirrel."

"I've never seen a black squirrel before," I said.

"The first time I saw Lucky," Bogey said, "I thought he was a small skunk, so I ran away fast. Randy chased after me and explained that Lucky was actually a black squirrel, not a skunk."

"Why did you run away?" I asked him, "Skunks are kind of cute when they waddle. Do they really smell that bad?"

Randy laughed and said, "I want to tell this story!"

He sat on his hind legs moving his front paws excitingly. We all sat down under Randy's tree and listened.

Once Randy had all of our attention he said, "Everyone in the woods knew what happened that day. Actually, we could all smell what happened."

"What did happen?" I asked Randy.

"We were walking through the woods when Bogey thought he saw a member of his family. He was so excited to think he may have found a brother or a sister."

Bogey interrupted and said, "I'm gonna tell this part. It's my story."

Randy eased back down on all four legs and said, "You're right, Bogey. You tell it."

"This creature was black all over with a little patch of white fur on his nose. He had a white stripe down his back, sort of like me." Bogey continued. "I rushed up to him, thinking he could be someone in my family. I put my paw on his back. I guess I startled him. He jumped and turned around. I knew then he didn't look like me at all. Randy backed away. I heard him laugh. He knew what was about to happen. I didn't. An awful smell surrounded us. I tried to breathe. The smell was so bad, it burned my nose. So I held my breath. Randy took off in a hurry. I ran as fast as my legs would go. Finally we stopped and sat down to catch our breath. Between laughs, Randy said, 'Now, my friend...you've just met a skunk!' "

"We didn't get near Bogey for days 'cause he smelled so bad," Wiggles giggled. "There's lots of funny stories about Bogey."

"You all have told enough stories about me," said Bogey. He got up, bowed his back up and stretched his legs out front.

"I want to hear more!" I begged.

"There are so many stories about Bogey, especially when he was a kitten. He got in a nasty cat fight once. He came home with a huge scratch on his nose and a nip out of his ear. I could tell you lots of tales about Bogey," said Randy.

From the gleam in his eye, I knew he wanted to tell me more.

"Not now, we don't have time," Bogey answered, "if we're going further into the forest to explore."

Wiggles looked up at the sky and sniffed the air.

"You going into the forest with a storm coming?" asked Wiggles. "You know you might happen to see The Gray…."

Bogey quickly clamped his paw over Wiggles' mouth.

"Who?" I asked. "What were you gonna say, Wiggles?"

"Oh, he's not saying anything," Bogey said and glared at Wiggles.

Randy swished his black striped tail. His mask looked like it might slip off.

"Oops! Sorry I mentioned it, Bogey," said Wiggles, "Gotta go."

"You three know a secret you aren't telling me." I said.

"No. Nothing. Nothing at all," Wiggles stuttered.

I stared at three guilty faces.

Ten

"All of you know a secret. I love secrets! Tell me," I begged. "Secrets? We don't know any secrets, Mattie," said Wiggles. "I gotta go. Mom told me I had to collect at least twenty acorns before the sun went down. We store them for winter. I've got to get started!"

"I'll help you tomorrow, Wiggles," Bogey said.

"I'll help you too," I chimed in. "I like to pick up nuts."

"Well, since we can't tell any more of your stories, Bogey, I'll go back to sleep on my favorite limb," said Randy. "Wiggles, don't make so much noise when you gather nuts. You always eat one and save one and your crunching wakes me up. And Mattie," he said with a grin, "I'll let you know if any fairies fly over me while I nap."

"Promise you won't eat them, Randy," I begged.

Randy giggled and said, "Course not, Mattie. Wouldn't dream of it. I'm a bit picky about what I eat. I don't want to choke on a fairy and her magical dust."

Randy scooted up to his limb high in the tree. Wiggles climbed behind him and grabbed nuts off the limbs, mumbling, "Can't help it if I smack when I munch my acorns."

Oak trees drop acorns once a year in the fall. Acorns are a great supply of food for animals, especially squirrels, bears, deer, and birds.

"I'd like to climb like Wiggles and Randy," I said with a sigh.

I looked down at my hands, wishing for claws of my own.

"If I had long fingernails, they might work like claws. What do you think, Bogey?"

"Nope. They wouldn't," Bogey said.

"Does Lucky like to climb trees too?" I asked.

"Of course he does. He's a squirrel," said Bogey.

"You said maybe we could go exploring in the forest. Can we go see Lucky, your black squirrel friend?"

"Lucky is probably in the old cemetery. There's a big tree there full of his favorite food. Are you sure you want to go? It's kind of spooky. It's further in the woods where it's a little darker. You might get scared."

"No, I won't. I like creepy things," I said as I crossed my fingers behind my back. "What's there to be afraid of? Ghosts?"

47

Bogey whispered, "Maybe."

I stood up tall and said, "I don't care. I'm not afraid of ghosts." *That wasn't exactly true.*

Bogey swished his tail. Water flew off the tip and landed on me. I brushed it off.

"I'd love to see a ghost," I said.

Bogey raised his eyebrows.

"I don't think you're telling the truth, Mattie," said Bogey.

I wasn't sure I was either. I tucked my head down and followed Bogey into the woods towards the cemetery. The wind picked up and whistled through the trees.

"If any fairies were in here, they would have been swept away," I said.

The leaves blew down along our path. My boots crunched twigs on the ground.

"Gee, Bogey, I sure hope I don't step on a fairy. How much further is it to the cemetery?"

We walked in silence.

"You never answer me," I said.

"Cause you ask too many questions," Bogey said.

The limbs on the trees swayed and birds were tossed off. They tried to fly, but bounced around in the air. Finally they flew back to the limbs and hung on tight.

I followed Bogey. His snake-like tail stood up straight and tall and was beginning to dry. It sorta looked like a flagpole now.

The trees were blowing so hard, the tops of them leaned into each other. They seemed to be talking to each other. They whistled to me. *Were they trying to warn me about something? Maybe we should turn back. But if I said anything, Bogey would think I'm scared. I'm not, am I?*

Something landed on my arm and I jerked away. Good, it was only a pinecone. A black shadow swooped by my face. Feathers brushed my cheek. I jumped back and screamed.

"S – Q – U – A – W – K!" screeched the black shadow as it soared in the air.

"That black thing tried to attack me, Bogey!"

I fanned my hand back and forth across my face trying to scare him off.

"Was that a bat? Bats suck blood out of you, don't they? He could have landed on my face and you didn't even see him. And I..."

"Mattie," Bogey interrupted, "That wasn't a bat. It was a crow. He won't hurt you."

"He could have if he'd hit me in the nose," I said. "He was going pretty fast. Everyone in here seems to be in a hurry and moving out."

Bogey shook his head and walked on.

I shivered. My bottom lip trembled.

"This place is kind of creepy, isn't it?" I said.

"You said you like creepy, remember?" said Bogey.

"I might change my mind," I said.

"Mattie, shh! Come on. We'll talk later," said Bogey. "Let's hurry if you want to see Lucky. I think Wiggles was right about a storm blowing in."

Bogey ran ahead winding around the tree trunks. My cowboy boots slowed me down. He squeezed through small spaces and under the bushes thick with all kinds of tangled up stuff. I didn't fit through and didn't want to. There could be spiders. I had to walk around and part the curtains of moss and vines that hung down in my face.

I mumbled to myself, "I was wrong to think fairies would want to live in here. They'd want more light and pretty flowers to dance on. There's not even any butterflies for them to play with."

Bogey stopped and turned back to me and asked, "Mattie, who are you talking to?"

"Oh, nobody," I said as I swatted a huge bug that had landed on my arm.

I looked around. My eyes darted left and right to see if anything or anyone was there.

Why did I have the feeling there was?

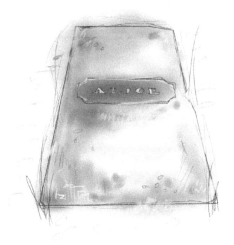

Eleven

We walked further into the forest. The sky darkened.

I leaned closer to Bogey and whispered, "Have you ever seen any ghosts in here?"

Bogey was silent.

We came to a clearing in the woods. A small path led to a huge iron gate.

"That's the entrance to the cemetery where Lucky lives," said Bogey.

"Looks like nobody ever goes in," I said. "It's surrounded by a huge brick wall."

Vines covered the wall and water oozed out between the cracks in the brick. Slime dripped on the mossy ground. Big stone columns held up iron gates to the entrance.

"Something's carved in the stone. I want to see what it says," I whispered.

"It's too high up for you to see, Mattie and it's covered in vines."

"Well I'm gonna read it," I insisted.

I shoved a big stone next to the column and climbed on top of it. It wobbled. I managed to pull the vines off the carving and brush away the green moss with my fingers. A cricket jumped on my hand.

"OH, NO….Go away cricket," I said.

I peered closer.

"I can see it now, Bogey. It's a date," I said. "And this place is really, really old. It's says 1740."

I hopped off the stone and stood next to Bogey. We looked through the gate.

I wrapped my hands around the bars of the gate and pressed my face against the cold iron. I squinted to get a better look at the cemetery. Giant trees stood tall like guards with their long limbs draped over the graves. *Were they protecting the dead?*

I pushed against the gate. It rattled, but didn't budge.

"This gate is ancient," I said. "How do we open it?"

"I don't know, if it's locked," Bogey said.

"We've come this far. We can't turn back now. I want to see Lucky. Can't you walk through the bars and I'll climb over," I suggested.

"Won't work," Bogey said.

"Why not?" I asked.

"For one thing, I can't fit between the bars in the gate. I already tried that one time."

"You're too wide, huh?"

"Guess so," he grinned.

"Can't you suck your stomach in and push through?" I asked.

"No, I can't," said Bogey. "I tried it once and got stuck. Lucky had a hard time pushing me through. But the wall's too high for you to climb anyway, Mattie."

"I'll put my arm through the bars and try to open it from the inside. It must open somehow," I said.

I reached my hand through the bars and tugged at the heavy bolt.

"It's rusty, Bogey and hard to lift, but give me a minute," I said determined.

"You don't have to do this," Bogey said.

"But I want to!" I said.

It took all my strength to lift the bolt. With a big clang, the latch released. I leaned on the gate and shoved it open. The heavy gate groaned. We stepped into the dreary cemetery.

"Good job, Mattie," Bogey said.

The wind blew harder. I looked up at the gray swirling clouds. It smelled like rain.

"It might storm, Mattie. You okay with that?" Bogey asked.

"Sure! I like storms," I mumbled, not paying much attention to what Bogey said.

I crept between the graves and looked around. I drug my hand across the top of a headstone. It was very cold. I turned my palm up. My fingers were dirty and green. Some of the tombstones were so old, they leaned against each other. They looked like real people made of stone. The ground was moist. My boots were quiet as I walked through the cemetery. I read the names of some of the dead people on the headstones.

"There are lots of people buried here, Bogey. They've been dead a long, long time," I said. "Most of the dates are, are... around 1800," I stuttered.

"This lady's name was Alice, Bogey," I said.

"Yeah, I know all about Alice. Randy told me."

"Told you what?" I asked.

"You make a wish and walk backwards around her tombstone thirteen times. I did it," he said.

"And did your wish come true?" I asked.

"Yeah, it sure did."

"What did you wish, Bogey?"

"I wished for a family of my own and that I would never be hungry again. My wish came true. I have a home with Nana and she feeds me everyday."

"I'm gonna make a wish and walk backwards thirteen times," I said.

"Okay, go ahead," said Bogey.

I closed my eyes and wished silently. *May Bogey and I become good friends and... Tucker not be mad at me for having fun with a cat.*

I slowly stepped backwards around Alice's grave.

"Don't tell me, Mattie," said Bogey. "It's your secret. You can't tell until it comes true."

"All right, I won't," I said. "One . . . two . . ."

I was almost finished with my thirteenth round when I tripped. I landed flat on my bottom. I looked up at Bogey. He sat there with his paws clamped over his mouth. He was trying hard not to laugh.

"Go ahead! Laugh!" I said.

"You're not too good at walking backwards, are you?" he chuckled.

"My boot caught on a big stick," I said.

I stood up, held my head high and carefully stepped backwards the rest of the way around Alice's grave.

"Yeah, I did it!" I shouted spinning around and clapping my hands over my head. My shouting echoed through the forest. I stopped and listened.

"*Yeah, I did it* . . ." I heard the sound of a faint voice return and fade away.

Chills ran down my back. I stood very still and looked at Bogey. His hair stood up on his back. I scrunched down beside him.

Alice is buried in an old cemetery on the coast of South Carolina. The plain marble slab on her grave has only one word - Alice. There are many tales and sightings of her ghost haunting the area.

"Was that my voice or Alice's? What do you think, Bogey? Could she be here and talking to us?"

"I don't know," said Bogey.

The cemetery was still and quiet, except for a ghostly wind rustling the trees.

Twelve

"Are you sure you want to keep going further into the cemetery?" Bogey asked.

Leaves floated through the air and brushed against my cheek. The hairs on the back of my neck bristled.

"Yes…, I want to keep on going. I'm NOT afraid." My heart thumped as I spoke.

"Could've fooled me!" Bogey said.

I twisted my curls around my finger again.

"Are you scared? You're twisting your hair," said Bogey.

"No!" I said.

I stomped my foot and quickly dropped my hand down by my side.

Moss hung low from the tree branches and swayed in the wind. It looked like long arms reaching down to grab me. Goose-bumps popped out all over my arms.

"Look, there's Lucky!" Bogey cried out. "Hi, Lucky!"

The black squirrel sat on his hind legs on an old tombstone covered with green moss. His fuzzy black tail blew in the wind. He held a big nut in his paw.

"Hi Bogey!" He answered back.

He put the nut in his mouth and it cracked.

Pieces of shell fell out of his mouth and he licked his lips. I crept over and sat on the cold stone next to him.

"Hi Lucky, Gee you're cute!" I said.

He turned to me with a mouth full of nuts, smacked and said, "You're pretty cute yourself, little miss, and brave too. Most people won't come into a creepy place like this, especially with a storm coming."

"Well, I wanted to meet you," I said. "What are you doing?"

"I'm collecting nuts for the winter," said Lucky.

"Looks like you're eating them to me," I grinned.

Lucky laughed and his fat tummy jiggled just like Wiggles' tummy had done.

"Yeah, I have a bad habit of doing that. Nuts are soooooo… good. Would you like one?"

Lucky held his paw out with a nut in it.

"No thanks, Lucky. I'm afraid I can't crack it like you do," I said. "Save it for winter."

Bogey jumped up on the tombstone next to me. He looked worried.

"This weather looks pretty bad. We really need to be on our way, Mattie."

"Not now, Bogey. I just met a black squirrel for the first time in my whole life. I don't want to go home."

I turned back to the black squirrel, "Lucky, you really do look a little bit like Bogey," *and a skunk too*, I thought to myself. "Have you seen any fairies in here and . . .?"

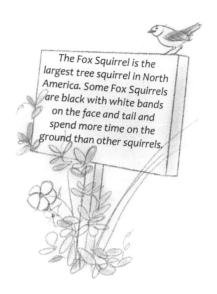

The Fox Squirrel is the largest tree squirrel in North America. Some Fox Squirrels are black with white bands on the face and tail and spend more time on the ground than other squirrels.

Bogey interrupted before Lucky could answer, "Lucky, with this storm coming have you seen The Gray . . . um . . ."

"You mean The Gray Man? Nope, not yet." Lucky shook his head and chewed nuts.

I leaned in closer to Lucky and said in a low voice, "Who's The Gray Man?"

The wind blew loudly. Thunder roared in the distance. There was a chill in the air.

"You don't know about The Gray Man?" Lucky asked surprised. "Everybody knows about him. He comes to warn people on the coast when a storm is coming. He always appears when we have a hurricane. He's a mysterious gray figure. Some say he's the spirit of a man who died here a long time ago."

"Whoa! You mean he's a ghost? A real ghost?" I blurted out.

My eyes opened wide. I was scared now. I started to twist my hair, but stopped. Instead I crossed my arms over my chest and looked around the cemetery.

"I saw him before the last storm," said Lucky. "He walked or rather, floated quietly through these graves and then he vanished. One of my friends said that sometimes he comes out of his grave and walks around. If you hang around a while, he may show up. He usually walks through the graves as if he's visiting the dead people. He's never noticed me."

"That's because you were scared and hid behind a tombstone," Bogey teased.

"I wasn't actually hiding. I was just spying on him," said Lucky.

"Yeah...right," laughed Bogey.

"Sh-sh-shouldn't we get going then, Bogey?" I stuttered.

"Oh, don't be a scaredy cat," said Lucky calmly. "The Gray Man has never hurt anybody."

"The story is he shows himself late in the afternoon on a stormy day," Bogey added. "Others say he only comes at midnight. But everybody says he's a good ghost. Isn't that right, Lucky?" Bogey asked with a little doubt in his voice.

I didn't give Lucky a chance to answer.

"Whatever kind of ghost he is," I stammered. "I changed my mind. I don't want to see him! Let's get out of..."

Thunder roared again and lightning skyrocketed across the sky. The whole cemetery lit up. I could see more than I wanted to see.

Before the scream could come out of my mouth, I heard a creepy noise. I turned slowly at what sounded like a squeaky door opening. Or was it a tombstone shifting or maybe a grave being opened? Chills went down my back. I whispered to Bogey, "What was that?"

Thirteen

ogey heard the noise. His back bowed up and his hair stood straight up. It made him look twice his size, and he was already pretty big. *How'd he do that?* He looked like a spooky Halloween cat. He lifted his cheeks and made a spitting noise. We heard another creak. Startled, the three of us jumped down behind a tall tombstone. Lucky's acorns scattered all over the ground. We huddled together with me in the middle. I scrunched down and tried to be as small as Bogey and Lucky.

"Why did you spit?" I glared at Bogey. "You could have spit on me! You looked so scary!"

"That's the point," he said. "It's supposed to frighten away anything that comes close."

I sure hope it did.

I whispered in his ear, "If only I hadn't acted so big and brave, you and I wouldn't be here now."

My stomach churned round and round. I felt like I had swallowed a bunch of butterflies.

"This wasn't a good idea, Bogey. Are you scared?"

He gave a slight nod and said, "It'll be okay, Mattie." He sounded a little unsure to me.

Lucky looked from left to right and behind us. "What do you think, Bogey?" he asked.

"Not sure," Bogey answered.

"Well, what I think," I said, "is we need to get out of here... fast."

"Hold on, Mattie," Lucky said.

Another creepy noise sounded.

I spun around.

"Where did that come from?" I asked. "Are there wild animals in here? Let's run! Which is the quickest way out of here? Which way do we go?"

It was quiet for a few seconds. Almost too quiet when a bolt of lightening struck a small tree. The tree split open. Sparks flew. With a loud moan, the tree cracked and snapped limbs. It slowly fell through the forest in our direction.

"Duck!" Bogey yelled.

I put my arms over the top of my head.

The ground trembled. Lucky scooted under my knees.

I heard the tree crash on top of the tombstone. Branches landed on us.

I felt a huge yell bubbling up in my throat. I shut my eyes and opened my mouth wide to scream.

A fuzzy paw plopped on my tongue. My eyes flew open.

"What...?"

"Be quiet, will you Mattie," Bogey whispered.

I pulled a hair out of my mouth and said, "What Bogey?"

He didn't look at me, but peeked around the fallen tree. Branches hid most of the tombstone.

"Can we escape? Are we pinned down?" I asked.

Bogey and Lucky didn't answer.

"What do you see, Bogey," Lucky asked. "Is it the ghost . . . The Gray Man?"

"Don't know yet."

Shuffle, shuffle... Shuffle, shuffle.

Oh . . . no. Is it him?

"Shh... Listen," I whispered.

Shuffle, shuffle...

"What is it?" I asked.

Huddled down under my knees, Lucky whispered, "I think that sound came from the chapel over there."

I pushed a limb aside and peeped out from around the tombstone. I looked at the small chapel.

"Someone's walking around in there. Maybe it's The Gray Man," I whispered.

"On the count of three, Bogey, let's run. I'll grab Lucky."

Bogey softly put his paw on my arm and sighed with relief, "Whew! It's okay, it's Sammy."

I stood up to peek over the top of the tombstone. I spread the leaves of the tree out of my way to get a better view. A gray figure of a man stood in the doorway of the church. Mist swirled around his feet.

"Is Sammy The Gray Man?" I whispered. "The ghost? I don't wanna see him. Let's go."

Bogey chuckled, "No, silly, he's the minister at the chapel."

"Hi, Bogey," the man yelled over the wind, "I saw you and your friends jump behind the tombstone when lightning hit the tree. Glad none of you are hurt. Bogey, you and your friends need to head home before the storm gets worse."

Bogey jumped out from behind the tombstone. He darted up the stone steps of the chapel. Sammy leaned down and petted Bogey. It looked like Sammy was talking to Bogey about something.

I looked at Lucky and said, "What's going on?"

Before Lucky could answer, Bogey rushed down the front steps of the chapel and said, "Mattie, crawl out from under the tree and let's start home. You okay, Lucky?" asked Bogey.

Lucky was still scrunched down under my boots. "Is it okay to come out now?" he asked with a tremble in his voice.

65

"Yeah, it is. It's Sammy, our friend," Bogey answered.

"Oh, good," smiled Lucky.

I reached down, picked up Lucky and moved him out from under me. I pushed the tangled tree branches off, stood up and looked towards the chapel.

"You must be Mattie," Sammy called out. "Your Nana told me you were visiting her. I'll see you another time Mattie," Sammy said. "I'll call the cottage and say the two of you are on your way. Hurry on now, before you get soaked. Bogey, I know you hate to be wet."

If only Sammy knew Bogey had already been soaked once today.

They seem to be good friends. I would have to ask Bogey how he knew Sammy.

We started to walk away but I stopped, looked back and waved to Sammy.

"Ya'll be careful and go straight home!" He called out.

"Yes sir, we will!" I hollered back.

I looked at Lucky, sitting on the ground surrounded by all of his nuts.

"Do you want to go home with us, Lucky? I'll help you pick up your acorns." I said, wanting his company. I would have a chance to ask him about the forest fairies. He must have seen some.

"No thanks. Not this time. I need to gather my acorns myself and take them home. You two need to hurry."

"Lucky's right, Mattie. Nana will begin to worry about us," said Bogey.

Bogey and I said good-bye to Lucky. I gave Lucky a pat on his head and he grinned. Bogey and I turned towards the iron gate.

The wind was getting stronger as we weaved our way along the old path.

I shuttered, "I sure don't want to meet THAT Gray Man on our way home."

We came to the open iron gate and this time went quickly through it.

"We ought to shut the gate, Mattie," Bogey said.

"Maybe The Gray Man will do it for us," I said.

"I don't think he shuts gates. He floats through them."

"Why didn't you tell me about The Gray Man when we talked about the cemetery?"

"I thought it might scare you," Bogey said.

"Well, it did," I said.

"Guessed that already," he nodded his head and grinned.

"Let's keep moving fast," I gasped, almost out of breath. "The gate's heavy and it's hard to close. We'll come back and shut it tomorrow."

Leaves blew down on top of us and covered the path.

Bogey sprinted ahead of me. It was hard to keep up because my cowboy boots slipped on the oak leaves and acorns. Before I could call out for Bogey to wait, "CRASH!"—something fell from one of the trees right behind me. The ground shook and so did I.

The earth seemed to groan.

Is The Gray Man pushing up the heavy stone on his grave? Did it knock over a tree?

I screamed, "Bogey! It's The Gray Man!"

The tip of my boot caught under a tree root. I stumbled and lost my balance. I fell flat on my face with a thud. Branches fell down on top of me and pinned me to the ground. The wind howled like a wolf. I didn't move a muscle, but managed to raise my head a tiny bit. Dirt and pine needles blew in my face. I cupped my hands over my eyes to shield them. I looked down the path for Bogey. I didn't see anything but a tiny lizard that slithered across the path in front of me.

"Please don't crawl my way," I whimpered. *Where was Randy, that raccoon when I needed him? Had Lucky already gone home too?*

"Lucky, Lucky are you here?"

No answer.

A spider web with a black spider blew out of the Spanish Moss. It fell across my left eye. I brushed it away.

"If you come near me, spider, I'll scream."

"Bogey, Bogey, where are you?" I whispered as loud as I dared.

I waited. There was no answer. I was all alone. My skin crawled.

Did Bogey get snatched by The Gray Man? Would The Gray Man take Bogey away to his grave? Could Bogey crawl out? Is The Gray Man gonna get me? I felt my heart pounding again. Lucky said he's a good ghost, but maybe he isn't. I looked for Bogey through the forest of trees. It was hard to see because the wind swept up the forest floor and swirled it high in the air. I watched and waited. The long swaying moss suddenly looked like dancing dead spirits. A tall, gray shadow surrounded by a whirlwind of leaves and pine needles stood in the middle of the path. The shadow slowly drifted in my direction. *Was that the ghost they call The Gray Man? Did he see me?* I didn't feel alone anymore but I sure didn't like who was here with me.

Since the plantation days of 1822, legends tell of The Gray Man, who walks among the dunes and live oaks to warn of an approaching storm.

Fourteen

After I saw the shadow, I shut my eyes tight. *Is that The Gray Man coming towards me? A real ghost? Am I pretending again? Please let me be pretending.*

I risked a tiny peep. It looked like a big gray mist. If I stay still, maybe The Gray Man won't see me. With the wind blowing so hard, he might float over me. Didn't Lucky say The Gray Man floated?

I buried my head in the mossy ground and closed my eyes. My face felt damp.

I'm not crying . . . , am I?

The wind came to a sudden stop. Quietness fell over the forest. I got an eerie feeling. Light footsteps rustled the leaves near me. I thought ghosts didn't make any noise, but something did. Someone was definitely there and getting closer. Was it a ghost? I couldn't look. Maybe that alligator came back for Bogey and me? I think I would choose the ghost. The branches and twigs on top of me moved a little.

Something bumped against my hair. I jerked my head up. My eyes flew open. Whew . . . ! Long, white whiskers tickled my cheek. I've never been so glad to see a fuzzy black and white face.

"Oh, Bogey, you saved my life!"

A little, pink nose brushed against my nose. I grinned.

"Actually, Mattie... I didn't."

"Bogey, I thought you'd left me with The Gray Man."

"No, Mattie. I wouldn't do that."

"Thanks for coming back, Bogey. I wouldn't have found my way home."

"What are you doing on the ground?" Bogey asked. "Are you hurt?"

"No, I tripped," I said, "I couldn't see and I thought The Gray Man was comin' to get me. I stayed still so he would float over me."

"There's a few branches on top of you, but I think you can get up," he said as he walked across my back and inspected the limbs that had fallen on me. My back sagged under his weight.

"Get up and brush yourself off. We need to get home," said Bogey.

I stood up and pulled leaves out of the new rip in my jeans. I put my hands in my hair and felt the gunk stuck in my curls. I pulled some out. My hand was full of wet leaves and pine needles.

Bogey rolled his eyes, lifted his cheeks and smiled. His whiskers moved up and down and his front teeth showed. I felt a lump in my throat. *Wow, he's so cute.* I tilted my head and held my hand over my heart. *I can't believe I thought that about a cat.*

A big grin spread over Bogey's face.

"What's so funny?" I asked.

"A lot of stuff is stuck in your hair. And if you get one more hole in those jeans they'll fall off." His grin got bigger. "You kind of look like a scarecrow. But come on. It's beginning to rain," Bogey said. "My fur had just begun to dry. It looks like I'm gonna get wet again if this storm doesn't blow out to the ocean."

"Look at the branches, Bogey. The wind is swaying them towards the ocean."

"You're right. They are," said Bogey.

We walked along in silence for a while. I couldn't quit thinking about the big crash and that gray shadow.

"Do you really think that was The Gray Man back there?" I asked Bogey.

"I don't know," Bogey said, "But he might be gone if the storm's blowing over. Were you scared, Mattie?"

"Well, uhhh, no not really," I tried to act brave, but had chills all over me. "Were you scared, Bogey?" I asked.

"I was a little bit," He admitted. "Let's not tell anybody about this, okay? It's embarrassing," Bogey said. "I don't want Wiggles, Lucky, and Randy to know I was scared. They'll tease me, and they do enough of that already. They've all seen The Gray Man. I'm the only one who hasn't and they love to point that out."

"Actually, that could have been The Gray Man back there," I answered. "Bogey, I really was scared," I confessed.

"We'll keep this our secret," Bogey said.

I zipped my finger across my chest twice, held my right hand up and said, "Cross my heart."

Bogey looked puzzled, and said, "Whatever."

We had walked a long way. My boots were heavy. "I've got to rest a minute, Bogey," I said and plopped down by a big tree.

"Mattie!" screamed Bogey.

"What?" I yelled.

"Wow, you just missed squishing that frog!" Bogey shouted.

I jumped straight up.

"Where is he?" I asked. "Oh! I see him. He's so small. Look at his little face. He must be hungry, don't you think?"

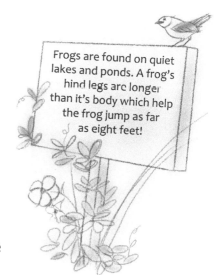

Frogs are found on quiet lakes and ponds. A frog's hind legs arc longer than it's body which help the frog jump as far as eight feet!

"Well, maybe" Bogey answered, "He'll find some bugs. You and I need to keep going."

I stood there with my hands on my hips.

"Bogey, I can't leave a starving frog!" I squatted down and stared at the frog. He stared back with sad eyes.

Slowly I eased my hand towards his head. He stuck his neck out and I petted him. He grinned at me. That did it.

"He's going with us," I said.

I stuffed him in my blue-jeans pocket.

"You're going to smash him!" Bogey yelled.

"No, I'm not. His head's sticking out. He's looking around. I think he likes it up here." I rubbed the frog's head gently.

"Can you walk with a frog in your pocket?" asked Bogey.

"Yeah, I can," I said.

"Okay then. Let's keep moving," said Bogey and walked off.

"He's kinda cute, isn't he Bogey?"

"Well, I guess he is," Bogey said over his shoulder. "I never thought about a frog being cute."

"He can be our new pet," I mumbled to myself.

I ran to catch up with Bogey and said, "Do you think he's ever seen a fairy?"

"Mattie, maybe you're just pretending in fairies."

"NO... I'm not!" I shouted.

Bogey flicked his tail, gave me a huff and didn't answer.

We walked on in silence. Finally, I said, "I don't think this looks familiar. Maybe we ought to go back and ride home with Sammy in his car."

"No, I hate to ride in cars. Sammy knows that," said Bogey.

"Is Sammy a good friend of yours?" I asked.

"Yes, a very good friend. He found me when I was lost and hungry. Sammy picked me up, petted me and made a bed for me in his church. Each morning in the garden, Sammy practiced his sermons as I sat next to him. I listened and learned that God created everything . . . trees, flowers and all the animals. He even made . . . ME!"

"Well, God did a really good job painting your face with black and white and giving you a little pink nose," I said.

Bogey looked puzzled.

"What?" I asked.

"I've never seen my face," said Bogey.

"I'm going to show you your face the first chance we get," I said as I patted his face.

"Randy says I'm a good lookin' cat," said Bogey as he pranced away with his big tail straight up in the air. It had dried and was bushy again. *He's so sure of himself.*

"Come on. Follow me, Mattie," he called over his shoulder.

"Do you think we're going in the right direction, Bogey? I don't remember any of this."

Bogey replied, "Well... cats can find their way home... most of the time. It's the storm that has me a little confused. The smells are different after the rain."

"Are we on the right path?" I asked.

"Not sure. I wouldn't say we're lost just yet. But you're right, Mattie.

"Why don't you climb a tree and see if you can spot the way home," I suggested.

"Good idea, Mattie."

He chose a big tree with lots of branches and struggled to reach the top. As he climbed, pieces of bark fluttered down to the ground. Bogey disappeared behind a big limb.

"Be careful, Bogey. Don't fall again," I yelled up to him.

A few leaves drifted down from the tree.

"Well, what do you see?" I shouted.

"Nothing... Nothing that looks familiar to me."

"So..., we ARE actually lost!" I sighed.

Fifteen

"Don't worry, Mattie. I'll think of somethin'," he called from the top of the tree. "I'll get us home."

Bogey climbed back down the tree. He was out of breath.

"Guess my weight is a little out of control," he said. "Haven't climbed in a while. My claws hurt."

"Why?" I asked

"I guess from pulling up my twenty pounds. I peeled a lot of bark off that tree."

"Yeah, I know," I giggled.

Bogey and I continued walking, not sure we were going in the right direction.

"Why do you keep looking up? You're slowing us down," Bogey said.

"I'm looking for fairies so I can show you one."

"Mattie, maybe you can see fairies and no one else can."

I threw up my hands and said, "Maybe, but I'm gonna keep lookin'."

"Whatever," said Bogey. He flipped up his tail and walked on. It looked like a huge feather pinned to the back of him. The breeze blew and rippled the tip of his tail over his back.

I laughed and said, "Bogey, do you have a spring on that tail? How do you get it to flip up like that?"

"It's a cat thing," said Bogey.

"What do you mean? Do you have a button you press or something or did someone teach you how to do that?"

"Mattie, will you hush? I'm trying to find our way home. I can't think with you asking me all these questions. Do you always have trouble being quiet?"

I clamped my lips together so I wouldn't talk.

Finally, Bogey said, "I think I know a shortcut that Randy told me about one time."

"Wait a minute. My sock's getting bunched up in my boots. I need to pull it up."

I reached down inside my boot.

"Ahhhhhh" I screamed and jumped from one foot to the other.

"What is wrong with you now?" asked Bogey.

"A huge spider crawled on top of my boot! I mean huge! He's just hangin' on and lookin' at me with a mean face."

I yanked off my boot and flung the spider, boot and all in the bushes.

"What'd you do that for? Now you've got to go find your boot. Don't be such a scaredy cat," Bogey replied.

I limped over to the bushes. My red boot was easy to spot in all the green stuff. The wet ground soaked the bottom of my sock.

"How can I be a scaredy cat? You're the cat," I said as I leaned over in the bushes to get my boot.

Bogey rolled his eyes. "Okay, Miss Smarty Pants," he said with a slight grin.

"You'd better check the frog. As much as you jumped around, he might have gotten smashed."

"I don't think so. I've been checking on him," I said.

I grabbed my boot out of the bushes.

"Let me get my boot back on," I called.

I leaned up against a tree and pulled my sock up tight. I held my boot up to look for the spider. He was gone. I tugged it back on.

Bogey walked over to me and stood on his hind legs with his paws on my knees. He inspected the frog hanging out of my pocket.

"He looks okay, Mattie."

"Yeah, I think so too. What shall we name him Bogey?"

"Whatever you say, Mattie."

"How 'bout Freddie?"

Bogey's paws went up in the air and he replied, "If you think so."

"Well, I like Freddie. He looks like Freddie to me."

"The name Freddie is fine. Come on, slowpoke. I think the short cut is over there by the pond."

We trotted along the path and climbed over the limbs that had fallen during the windstorm. The sun came out and sparkled through the trees. I searched the trees to see if any fairies might have come out after the storm.

Bogey sniffed the air, smiled and said, "I think I smell the pond."

We heard a splash.

"We must be close, Bogey. That sounded like a fish jumping out of the water. It wasn't the alligator, was it?" I asked with a shaky voice.

"No. It might have been the otter who lives in that pond." Bogey pointed with his paw.

"An otter? Can I see him?"

"You might if he's swimming around when we cross the dam."

I looked across the pond.

"Are we going to cross THAT? It looks like a rickety bridge to me." I said.

"It's not a bridge. It's a dam." said Bogey. "I went across it once with Randy. But you'll have to watch where you step, or you'll fall."

"I'm not a scaredy cat. I can do this," I said and took a deep breath.

The dam was made of sticks and logs that had washed up into a big pile. Bogey started across.

"Wait a minute. I want to look for the otter. Do you see him?"

Bogey scanned the pond and said, "See that little head swimming around. That's an Otter."

"It is? I wish he'd come out of the water so I can see all of him. Tell him to come out, Bogey."

"No, he won't. Not now, anyway. He's busy chasing his supper. Finding food is the most important part of an animal's day, just like it used to be for me."

"I wish we had some food to give him," I said.

"It looks like he's having good luck. Let's go Mattie. Follow me."

Bogey walked gracefully winding his way to the other side of the dam.

I took a step onto the dam and wondered if it would hold me. After all, I weigh a little more than Bogey.

The Otter has built in nose plugs and earplugs for diving underwater. Its strong claws and webbed feet help the otter to catch crawfish, frogs and fish.

"I'm coming. I'm coming," I hollered and took a big step.

The dam seemed strong. I was almost across when my left foot dropped down. Something cracked. My boot sunk between the logs. I tried to lift my foot. It wouldn't come out.

"Bogey! Help! My boot's stuck! It's halfway in the water."

"Well, pull it out, Mattie," Bogey yelled from the other side of the dam.

"I can't. It won't budge."

"Well, yank it," Bogey hollered.

I yanked and my foot came out of the boot. I wobbled trying to keep my balance on the logs.

"Bogey, I'm going to fall in!"

"If you slip," he grinned, "You'll get a real close view of the otter."

"I don't want to be that close to the otter," I yelled across the dam.

"Can you swim, Mattie?"

"Course I can," I yelled back.

I lifted my left foot up in the air. My sock dripped with water. I tried to steady myself on my right boot. I wiggled back and forth and almost joined the otter in the pond.

Then I remembered seeing how the tightrope walkers in the circus kept their balance. I held my arms out from my sides and stood up straight. It worked. I was steady now. Slowly I stooped down and reached between the logs for my boot. Something slithered through the water. I jerked my hand back. It was something long and slimy.

Sixteen

I peered in the water in search of the long, slithery creature I'd seen.

Where is he?

I looked closer and screamed.

"There he is, Bogey. Come look! A snake is swimming around my boot! It's a big one!"

"Back up slowly, Mattie and move away from the snake. It could be dangerous."

"Well, maybe. Maybe not. A man brought a good snake to our school. I petted it. He showed pictures of a dangerous snake. I bet this one's a good one. He likes my boot. We could take him home to Nana." I bent down to get a better look. I pressed my hand against my pocket to hold Freddie in.

"Don't jump out now, Freddie. There's a snake here and snakes like to eat frogs."

"Mattie, PLEASE move away from the snake," Bogey called.

"I'm going to look at his markings.... Oh, Bogey, he's a rude snake."

"How do you know he's rude?"

"Cause he's sticking his tongue out at me and hissing. I don't want a rude snake."

I kept my eyes on him and Bogey continued to yell at me, "Mattie, get away NOW!"

"Oh, he's trying to go inside my boot. If he thinks he's going to live in my boot, he's wrong."

"Mattie, back up quickly," Bogey pleaded.

"No, I'm mad now. This is my only pair of cowboy boots."

I leaned down and grabbed the top of my boot. I twisted back and forth trying to wedge it from the logs. As I tilted my boot, water poured in carrying along the big snake. With a quick yank, I jerked my boot out of the logs.

Water snakes can be mistaken for the poisonous copperhead because of the similar brown markings. Expert swimmers and divers, water snakes feed on fish, frogs, and toads.

"I've got my boot Bogey, and the snake's inside."

Bogey's black fur turned almost white.

I raised my boot up high.

"Do you want to see him, Bogey?"

"No, no I don't," he hollered. Get rid of him. Quick!"

I poured the water and snake into the crack between the logs.

84

"Well, that takes care of that rude snake," I said, as I looked at my frog. "I hope you weren't scared, Freddie. I wouldn't let that snake eat you."

"Walk towards me, Mattie," said Bogey. "Don't bother to put your boot on. Just walk quickly. That snake might come back out."

"I'm coming, Bogey, but it's hard in my wet sock. It keeps getting snagged on the logs."

With my boot in my hand, I took baby steps across the dam and hobbled to the other side. Freddie's leg swung from side to side against my pocket. His wide eyes stared up at me. I was glad to step on ground that didn't wiggle.

"Ribbet, ribbet."

"What's wrong Freddie?"

Freddie answered with another tiny "Ribbet."

"Freddie's real nervous," I said. "I can tell he knows that snakes eat frogs. Do they chew them up or just swallow them whole?"

My pocket tickled me. Freddie squirmed and buried his head deeper in my jeans pocket.

"Sorry Freddie. We won't talk about the snake anymore," I said.

I sat down on a fallen tree stump and pulled my boot on.

"Ewwww! It's all squishy," I said.

"It'll dry," said Bogey.

I stood up and stared at the pond. I could see my reflection in the water.

"Come here, Bogey." I stooped beside him. "Look in the pond and you can see your face."

He did and jumped back.

"Wow . . . is that me?" he asked as he looked up at me.

"Yeah, it is," I said. "Take another look."

He peered in the water again and said, "Randy was right. I am a good lookin' fellow."

I glanced around hoping to get a glimpse of the otter again. Instead, I saw what looked like big bumps lined up on a tree that had fallen halfway in the water. The big bump crawled further up the tree. I squinted my eyes. The little bump moved.

"Wow! They're turtles. Look, Bogey! There's a momma, daddy and two baby turtles."

"Yep, I've seen them before. They like to sun themselves." Bogey said.

"They're so cute! I'll bet they're friendlier than that rude snake. Can you believe how rude he was? He was making spitting noises and stuck his tongue out at me. The snake at school didn't act like that. Do you think maybe he was having a bad day? And you acted like you were having a bad day. You were yelling at me about the snake. Why? Were you scared of him?"

Turtles are cold-blooded animals. They like to sun themselves to keep warm. A turtle can pull its head directly into the shell for protection.

"Yes, 'cause one bit me on my cheek," Bogey explained. "It started swelling right away. By nightfall, my head was as big as a pumpkin."

"It was? Was it orange? Did your whiskers turn orange? Did you look like a real pumpkin, Bogey?"

"Mattie, do you know how much you talk? You even talk to yourself. And when you talk, you don't walk. Will you please hush for a little while? You're such a slow poke."

I stomped on past him to show I could walk, not talk and wasn't a slowpoke. I was quiet for as long as I could stand it. I walked and walked.

"Can I talk now?" I called over my shoulder as I kept walking.

Bogey didn't answer.

I stopped quickly and turned around. Bogey wasn't there.

"Bogey? Where are you?"

No answer.

I jogged back down the path to look for Bogey. I ran through the tangle of trees weaving back and forth. No Bogey. The storm was over and everything was calm and still. The only sound was the breeze that rustled through the trees.

"Bogey?" I called out again.

He didn't answer.

The only sound I heard was my voice growing dimmer as it echoed back through the live oak trees.

Boooooooooogeeeeeeeeey, Booooooooogeeeeeeeey.

Seventeen

I heard a faint "meow".

I ran around a big tree. There was Bogey on the ground.

"You called *me* a slowpoke? Look at you! What are you doing lying here? Are you taking a catnap?" I asked.

Then I saw him licking his paw.

"Are you okay?" I asked and rushed over to him.

"I got a splinter in my paw crossing the dam," he said. "I tried to pull it out with my teeth but couldn't."

"Let me see it."

I stooped down and picked up his paw. The splinter was buried deep between the pads of his foot.

I pulled it, careful to be gentle like mom does when I get a splinter. Bogey didn't make a sound. I couldn't say the same for me. I always yell.

"You're brave, Bogey. It's almost out. There you go. You'll be all better now," I said.

"Thanks, Mattie. It already feels better." He limped a little as we walked away.

I looked up through the tree limbs at the white clouds swirling in the sky. Instead of fairies, I spotted two bluebirds perched on a limb.

"Look Bogey." I pointed to the birds. "Wow, those birds are bright blue! Aren't they cute with their feathers all puffed up. They look like they have little hats on. I guess they grew extra feathers to get ready for winter."

"You two lost?" one of them asked.

"No, we're not lost," said Bogey.

"Oh, yes, we are!" I shouted up to the birds.

I felt a pop on the back of my leg. I looked down.

Bogey's eyebrows scrunched together. He stared at me with an evil eye.

"Well, we're not really lost, just a little bit confused," I yelled up. I reached down, patted Bogey's head and said, "It's okay. I know you'll find the way."

"We're looking for our cottage by the marsh," said Bogey.

"We were just there," one bird said as he pointed his right wing. "We ate sunflower seeds at the birdfeeder and took a dip in the birdbath."

"Come back anytime," Bogey called out as we walked in the direction the bird had pointed.

"You two look a little pitiful. Are you all right?" One of the bluebirds asked.

"We're fine. We were just exploring the cemetery when the storm came up," said Bogey.

"You were at the cemetery?" He flapped his wings, stretched his neck out and lowered his beak. "Was... was The Gray Man there?" he whispered.

"Didn't see him," Bogey said.

"I might have seen..." I started to say. I felt a tap on the back of my leg.

"You crossed your heart not to tell," whispered Bogey.

"Well, I was just gonna tell the birds," I said in a low voice. "Even the bluebirds know about The Gray Man."

"Hush and let's keep going," said Bogey. "Thanks for your help," he called up to the birds.

I walked in the direction the bird had pointed. My steps were slower 'cause my boot was wet and heavy. Bogey limped behind me. The heel of my foot ached like I was getting a blister. I began to limp like Bogey.

"Guess we do look pitiful," I giggled.

Bogey grinned at me and said, "I don't know who looks worse. You or me?"

"You!" I said.

"Come on slowpoke. Keep moving," said Bogey.

I smelled the marsh and knew we were getting close to home.

We walked out of the woods into a clearing. Right in front of us was the marsh and the Blue Heron stood in the water.

"There's that bird we saw this morning," I pointed. "He's standing in the water. His legs must be three feet long. His tummy isn't even getting wet. Do you think he might be hungry? I hope he doesn't spot Freddie. I'd better stick his foot back into my pocket and cover up his head with my hands."

"Mattie, that bird's not going to fly over here and eat your frog," said Bogey.

"Well, he's getting ready to eat something. He's dropped his head. Look!" I screamed. "He's got a snake in his mouth. Do you think it's that rude snake we met?" I hopped around trying to get a better view.

The Heron lifted his long head up and stretched his neck towards the sky. Down went the snake like a piece of spaghetti.

"Oh, wow! That was gross, wasn't it Bogey? I'm glad Freddie didn't see that. Did he chew him up? Is he still alive swimming in his stomach?"

Bogey turned around and his eyebrows went up. He shook his head and walked off.

"How does she come up with stuff like that?" Bogey mumbled.

"Well, I just wondered if the snake was still alive," I shrugged.

My pocket twitched. I looked at Freddie.

"Are you okay? I wouldn't let that bird eat you." I took his foot back out and let it hang down. I could tell he liked that. He had a little grin on his face.

"Are you through talking now because we're almost to Randy's tree. I don't want you to wake him up. We already did that earlier," said Bogey.

We saw the big tree where I had first met Randy, the Raccoon. I looked up and sure enough Randy was sound asleep high up in the tree.

"Shhhh!" Bogey hushed. "Be quiet, Mattie or we'll wake him, and he won't be in a good mood."

"Where's your squirrel friend Wiggles?" I whispered.

"He's probably tree hoppin'," said Bogey.

"Tree hoppin?" I asked.

"All the squirrels have a highway through the trees," Bogey said. "They use it everyday to collect their nuts."

I squinted up at the tree branches and searched for the squirrel highway. And there it was! Squirrels ran along the huge limbs that spread from one tree to another.

Bogey darted ahead of me as I tip-toed around Randy's tree so I wouldn't wake him up. I watched where I stepped, being careful not to snap a twig and wake Randy.

"Come back, Bogey," I whispered. "Look at these tracks. What are they?"

Bogey hurried towards me. His golden eyes were wide with curiosity.

"Those are deer tracks," he whispered.

"How do you know?"

"I know deer tracks when I see them, Mattie."

"Really? Do you play with deer Bogey?"

"Not really, but I see them every night when they come out to nibble leaves on our bushes. I rub up against their legs to let them know that they're safe in our garden."

"Are the tracks fresh, Bogey? I don't remember seeing them earlier."

"Yeah, they're fresh tracks, all right. I can still smell the deer scent. If you can be very quiet, which seems to be hard for you, we might spot him."

I clapped my hands across my mouth to make sure I wouldn't speak a word.

I followed Bogey holding my hands to my mouth. I looked from left to right for the deer. Bogey's soft paws didn't make a sound. But my heavy boots crunched on every leaf and twig.

Bogey turned around and gave me a nasty look as if to say I was making too much noise.

"I'm trying to be quiet," I whispered.

At that exact moment, my boot snapped a twig. A rabbit with a white tail ran out of the bushes next to me.

"There's Peter Cottontail!" I yelled.

"I don't know Peter and you don't know how to be quiet!" He said with a frown and flipped his tail and walked off.

Out of the corner of my eye, I saw the Whitetailed Deer in the distance as it galloped away. His white tail stood straight up and had a tiny wiggle as he ran.

"Oh, Bogey, I wanted to pet him. When I saw Peter, I screamed and frightened the deer."

"That deer was going to run away whether you had made a noise or not. He heard us long before we saw him."

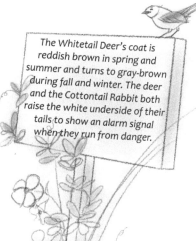

The Whitetail Deer's coat is reddish brown in spring and summer and turns to gray-brown during fall and winter. The deer and the Cottontail Rabbit both raise the white underside of their tails to show an alarm signal when they run from danger.

"The rabbit was cute, but he scared me when he jumped out of the bushes. Do you know Peter, Bogey?"

"Don't think I've ever met the fellow," said Bogey.

"Too bad. He's a cute rabbit," I said.

Bogey walked on and I could tell his right paw was beginning to bother him where I removed the splinter. He stopped to rest by two trees that had a rope hammock hanging between them. Behind the hammock was a tiny cottage across from Nana's house.

The doll like cottage was draped with long tree limbs that hung over it. The sun shone through the leaves and a slight breeze blew.

I screamed, "There they are, Bogey. Finally! There they are!"

"What? Who?"

Eighteen

"There they are Bogey!" I continued to scream. "They're here!"

"Who? What are you shouting about?" asked Bogey.

"The fairies, silly! Up there!" I pointed. "In the tree, right there!"

Bogey looked up and turned round and round, trying to spot them.

"I'm dizzy," he said as he plopped on the ground. "Mattie, are you imagining things again?"

"No, I'm not. They're dancing and they're all dressed in pink."

Bogey batted his eyelashes and squinted as if to clear his eyes. "Are you talking about the pink blossoms on the Mimosa tree?" asked Bogey.

"They're fairies!" I insisted, "…aren't they?"

We both walked closer to the tree and Bogey said, "Pull a limb down and look at the pink blossom."

Careful not to hurt the fairy, I plucked a small limb and stared at the pink skirt.

"This looks just like a fairy," I said as I twisted and turned the limb in my hand, "but ... it's not," I sighed.

I took a deep breath and moaned.

"Oh. . . . This is exactly what fairies look like. See their little pink skirts," I said as I squatted down close to Bogey.

Bogey looked at the flower I held right under his nose. I brushed the blossom back and forth under his nose.

"That tickles," he said. He threw his head back, sneezed hard and blew the skirt off the blossom.

The Mimosa Tree has beautiful silky pink blossoms that look like pompoms. This tree has low spreading branches with lacy like leaves.

"Wouldn't you love to have a pink skirt like the one you just blew away?" I asked Bogey.

"Cats don't like pink skirts, Mattie. Besides, it'd be too tight on my tummy," he answered and walked away.

I followed and stopped to look back at the tree with the pink blossoms.

"That's such a pretty tree, Bogey."

"Yeah, it is. It bloomed longer this year than ever before. But the blossoms are beginning to drop."

The tiny cottage underneath was covered in the petals that had fallen on top of it. I shook my head. They still looked like fairies to me.

"Is the little house yours, Bogey?" I asked.

"No, that's the guest house."

"I wish it was your house," I said. "So we could play in it."

"But the hammock looks like fun. Can we swing?" I begged. "I love to swing in hammocks!"

"Cats don't like to do that. It makes us dizzy and we might fall on our backs," he said.

"I'll hold you tight and you won't fall out, okay? Pleeeaaase?"

With a turn of his head, and a flip of his big bushy tail, he limped ahead of me and said, "I'm hungry and we need to go home."

"How can you think of your stomach at a time like this, when I really want to swing?" I caught myself beginning to whine and stopped.

"All right, Bogey. I'm sorry. I know your foot's hurting. I'm coming, I'm coming," I said, and limped on behind him.

When we almost got to the cottage, I eased Freddie out of my pocket and looked him over to make sure he was okay.

"He looks fine, Bogey. Don't you think so?"

"Yep. I do. Let's put him by the pond. He'll have lots of bugs to eat. Frogs love bugs," said Bogey.

"Look! The lightening bugs are coming out. Freddie won't eat 'em, will he, Bogey?"

"Don't think so," Bogey said.

"Would he light up if he did eat 'em?" I asked.

"Mattie, you know what?"

"What?"

"I have no idea," said Bogey.

Bogey limped over to the small pond close to Nana's house and pointed with his paw.

"Put him here, Mattie."

I gently put Freddie down.

Bogey patted Freddie's head with his paw and said, "See ya, Freddie" and hobbled towards Nana's cottage.

Freddie grinned at me and said, "Thanks for the ride."

I stared at Freddie.

"Wow! Why didn't you talk to me all day long?" I asked.

"For one thing, my name isn't Freddie and you called me that all day long. My name is Ellie. The other thing is I was afraid. I didn't know what you were gonna do with me. That's why I wanted to hang my foot out of your pocket, in case I needed to get away. You might have fed me to that big bird."

"Oh, I would never do that, Freddie. Oh, I mean, Ellie. Do you feel safe here?"

"Course I do. You'd better go now with your friend, Bogey. His foot's hurt."

"Bye, Ellie. Good luck with your bugs. When I hear that frog noise, I'll know it's you," I said.

"You mean when I go, 'ribbet, ribbet'."

"Yeah! That's it! Why do frogs do that?" I asked.

"Oh, just having a little fun and talking to other frogs."

"Well, stay away from the marsh," I said. "There's alligators and big herons in there."

"Don't worry about me," said Ellie.

"We'll see you tomorrow," I said.

I caught up with Bogey and looked back to wave to Ellie.

"Do frogs eat dead bugs or live bugs. What do they taste like, Bogey? Have you ever eaten a bug?"

"Course I did when I was hungry and lived in the woods. They aren't too bad."

I wrinkled my nose and said, "Sounds yucky to me. Maybe, just maybe, I would try one if you picked the perfect one for me. What would the perfect one look like, Bogey? Would it be red like a ladybug? Would it taste like chicken?"

"Please, Mattie. No more questions. I'm hungry and I'm sure cookies are waiting for you. You'll probably like them better than bugs. Come on. I'm beginning to feel tired and grumpy."

Bogey limped on ahead.

I ran to pick him up.

"Bogey, I know your foot hurts. Let me carry you the rest of the way home."

"You don't have to do that Mattie. I can walk."

"But I want to. I scooped him up with all my strength and said, "Wow, Bogey. You're one heavy cat!"

"Yeah, I am. I enjoy my food," he chuckled.

I shifted Bogey's weight so his head could look over my left shoulder. I used both hands to hold up the rest of him and there was a lot of him. I felt like I was carrying a twenty-five pound bag of dog food.

I groaned a little bit and said, "Are you comfortable now, Bogey?"

"Yeah, this is kind of fun up here. I can see a lot more than down on the ground. We'll have to do this more often," he said.

"Bogey, about your fall in the birdbath . . ." I said.

"What about it?" he asked.

"Uh . . . well . . . ," I struggled to get the words out.

Bogey turned his head and stared at me.

"I'm sorry I made you fall," I blurted out. "And I'm sorry I didn't say it earlier."

"It's okay, Mattie. I'm glad you said it now," he said.

I gave him a light squeeze and asked, "How old are you, Bogey?"

He didn't answer for a minute.

"I don't know," he finally said.

"Well, when was your last birthday party?"

"My what?" he asked.

"Bogey, we're going to have a birthday party for you and we're going to invite Randy, Wiggles, Lucky, Sammy, and Nana. How 'bout that?"

"Sounds like fun, I guess. What's a birthday party?"

"A party to celebrate the day you were born."

"But I don't know the day I was born."

"We'll make it up. Maybe my birthday can be yours too."

"Okay, but when is your birthday?"

"July 29."

"That's awfully hot for a party," said Bogey.

"How do you know it's hot in July, Bogey?"

I grinned and looked down at him and saw something red on my shirt. There was blood covering my shirt.

"Oh my, Bogey! You're bleeding."

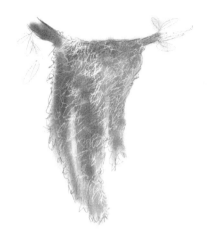

Nineteen

Bogey's paw was hurt.

"Mattie, I know I'm heavy. Put me down," said Bogey. "This morning you said you didn't like to pick up cats. Let me walk."

I struggled a little to shift his weight but said, "Like you said to me lots of times, 'HUSH! Don't talk anymore!' Speaking of talk... Uh... do you? Uh... can Nana?"

"Just say it, Mattie."

"Guess I was thinkin'... uh... do you and Nana... talk?" I blurted out.

"No, Nana and I understand each other... without speaking a word."

"Maybe we can keep our talking a secret," I said. "Like we're gonna do with The Gray Man, right?"

"Right. If that's what you wanna do."

"Now we have two big secrets!" I shouted, "Actually three! The third one is I'm gonna have a surprise birthday party for you." I danced around holding Bogey.

Bogey raised his cheeks and his teeth showed. He giggled.

"Bogey, you're a lot like me and I like me," I said and we both laughed.

I reached up and grabbed a strand of moss that hung low on one of the oak trees. I draped it around Bogey's head and made him a long gray beard.

"Now Bogey you're an old cat."

I skipped along holding Bogey to my chest and sang loudly, "HAPPY BIRTHAY TO YOU! HAPPY BIRTHAY TO YOU! HAPPY..."

Bogey laughed and covered his ears with his paws. I stopped singing.

"What's wrong?" I asked as I pulled the moss away. "Did a bug or lizard crawl in your ears?"

"No," he said. "It's your singing!"

"Guess my voice didn't sound too good. But it's hard to sing when I'm carrying a heavy cat . . . and dancing," I said.

"At least you sound better than Randy. He belted out 'Jingle Bells' one Christmas from his perch in the tree and all the birds flew away. Wiggles and I ran," said Bogey.

I threw my head back and laughed.

I climbed the cottage steps two at a time with my heavy bundle of cat.

I stood on the porch and looked at the wicker sofa. I noticed the dent in the cushions where Bogey had slept this morning. I turned around and looked back at the forest.

The sun sparkled behind the giant oak trees turning the leaves a pale gold. The Spanish moss gently swayed in the breeze. Small, gray wisps of moss slowly drifted to the ground. I took a deep breath, smelled the fresh air and looked at the blue sky. Clouds swirled around making animal shapes. I saw a squirrel, a big bird and . . . then the clouds drifted away.

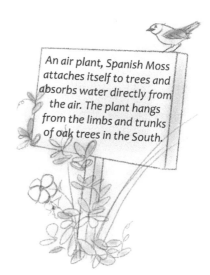

An air plant, Spanish Moss attaches itself to trees and absorbs water directly from the air. The plant hangs from the limbs and trunks of oak trees in the South.

I glanced at the birdbath. Two birds dipped their heads under, fluttered their wings and I almost thought I heard them giggle. The pink Mimosa tree still swayed in the breeze. The hammock gently rocked as if the fairies were swinging. The big heron squawked and rose up from the marsh with a fish in his mouth. Acorns dropped on the porch's tin roof with a "P I N G" and rolled to the ground. On tiptoes, I peeked at the pond. A quiet ribbet echoed back to me.

A warm fuzzy feeling spread all over me.

"Thanks Bogey."

He flipped his head around and stared in my eyes with a puzzled look on his face.

"Thanks for what?" he asked.

I hugged him tightly to my chest and gave him a good squeeze.

"Gosh, Mattie! You're squashing my stomach," said Bogey.

"Sorry," I said, and gave him a big kiss on the top of his furry head.

I shifted his weight so I could reach the door handle. I kicked the door open with my boot and went in.

"I'm glad you could open it cause I can't," said Bogey.

"I'll teach you how to open a door. You teach me about the animals."

"What do you wanna know?" asked Bogey.

"Everything," I said.

I smelled Nana's cookies, but they would have to wait. Bogey's paw needed doctoring first.

"I'm going to wash your foot in the kitchen sink, so don't fuss about it," I said.

"Mattie, cats lick their own wounds. You don't have to do this."

"Well, I'm gonna," I insisted.

"Oh, gosh I hate this," Bogey said as I put him in the sink. He tried to climb out, but I held on.

"Don't kick me. Hold still and quit wiggling, Bogey. I'm gonna get the water warm and it will only take a minute. It might even feel good."

I turned the facet on and Bogey started squirming again.

"Will you please be still?" I said. "You're a big boy. You can handle this."

"But I don't like it," said Bogey.

"I know. I know you don't."

I held his paw gently in my palm under the water and carefully rubbed it clean.

"Okay. You've done it. Put me down now, Mattie. I'll finish cleaning it later."

With a groan, I lifted him out of the sink and set him on the floor.

"All done. Let me dry it off with Nana's kitchen towel," I said.

I patted it softly.

"Now, it's all better. Let's get you some fresh water and supper. Where does Nana keep your food?"

"There in the pantry." Bogey limped over to the two doors and bumped his head on the left one.

I opened it. "There. There's my food," he said.

"Which one do you want, Bogey? There's lots of choices."

"I'll let you choose for me tonight," he said.

It was a hard decision. There were so many cans.

"Hmm… I choose turkey with gravy, if that's okay with you," I said.

"Sounds wonderful," Bogey said as he rubbed against my leg.

I pulled the top off the can.

"It smells so good. Hurry," said Bogey.

"You're right. It does smell good. Sort of like Thanksgiving dinner."

I emptied the can into Bogey's dish. He bumped his head on my hand.

"I like your dish Bogey, with this little fish painted on the bottom. Looks like my fish, Gus."

"It's kind of silly, but your Nana thinks it's cute."

Bogey lapped up his turkey and gravy.

"Guess you like my choice, huh? Gee, Bogey. Can you ever smack," I said.

Bogey kept smacking, shrugged and said, "Can't help it."

Footsteps sounded down the hall.

"Mattie, is that you?" asked Nana, "Who are you talking to?"

"Uh, oh, Bogey. Did Nana hear you talk?" I whispered.

Twenty

"I'm . . . I'm . . ." I stammered. "I'm in here, feeding Bogey, Nana. Just mumbling to myself."

I squatted down next to Bogey.

"Is our secret blown?" I whispered.

Bogey shook his head back and forth.

Nana rushed in the kitchen and stopped. Nana looked from me to Bogey.

"Oh my!" she exclaimed.

"What?" I asked.

Finally, a big grin spread across Nana's face.

"Everything must have gone well for you two today," she said. "You both look a mess." She laughed and pulled a few leaves out of my hair.

"Ouch," I said.

"Well, you kinda look like a fairy. A beautiful forest fairy," said Nana.

"Wow, Nana? Do you think the fairies would really think that?"

"Yes, I believe they would," answered Nana.

"I love fairies, Nana."

"Yes, I know you do."

Bogey looked up from his bowl and rolled his eyes. Nana missed seeing that, but I didn't and laughed out loud.

"I'm glad you had fun today, Mattie," said Nana.

She gave me a big hug and said, "You've got goose bumps on your arms. You're cold. Come sit by the fire and bring the cookies."

"Can I have one now, Nana? Pleeeese."

"Course you can. I made them for you."

I bit into the cookie.

"Mmmm... yummy."

Nana walked out of the kitchen and I followed munching my cookie. She sat down and I plopped at the foot of her chair.

I grabbed another cookie off the plate, took a big bite and crumbs dropped in Nana's lap. She didn't seem to mind, but I brushed them off anyway.

"Mattie, you did have a fun time today, didn't you?" Nana said, "I just knew you and Bogey would become good friends."

I lowered my head and said in a quiet voice, "You were right, Nana."

She leaned over and hugged me and I said, "I'd love to come back and go exploring with Bogey again."

"Is this the same granddaughter who this very morning, didn't like cats and thought the woods might be boring?" Nana teased.

With a shrug of my shoulder, I shyly said, "Yep, that's me. And Nana, will you help me find a tee shirt with a black and white cat on it?"

She laughed out loud and said, "We'll find one, I'm sure."

I heard a tiny noise and turned to look. Bogey walked in and sat by the fire.

"Bogey, you have some turkey on your mouth," I said.

He licked it off.

Whoops! I forgot our secret, so I changed the subject quickly.

"Nana, do you and Bogey…?" I hesitated and looked at Bogey.

"Yes, Mattie? What were you gonna ask me?"

"Nana, do you two go fairy hunting?" I blurted out.

Bogey dropped his head between his paws.

"No, Mattie. Bogey doesn't pretend in fairies like you and I do. Did you see any fairies today?"

"No, but I looked all day long."

Bogey looked up from me to Nana.

He got up and rubbed against Nana's leg. Then he climbed up on me and snuggled down in my lap. I petted him softly and felt his warm tummy against mine.

"It's a cool night, Nana. Can I sleep with Bogey? He would be cuddlier than my stuffed cat pillow."

Bogey looked at me with a funny look on his face.

"Bogey seems to have a question about your other cat," grinned Nana.

"Bogey, that cat isn't a real cat. It's made out of cotton. I use it for a pillow," I said to him. "It's not a real, live, pretty cat like you."

Did Nana know he understood what I said?

I calmly stroked Bogey's head and he settled back down into my lap. All three of us were quiet. The only sound was the fire that made a soft crackle as ashes fell down in the hearth. Bogey yawned and I could see halfway down his throat. I watched as Bogey's eyes started to close.

I bent down close to his ear and whispered, "Bogey, a beautiful fairy just lit on the top of your head."

His eyes flew open.

"You can't see her," I said, "Cause she's right between your ears. She's sprinkling her magic fairy dust all around you. You'll go to sleep and have wonderful dreams."

Bogey closed his eyes again and started purring.

Nana watched us and smiled.

"Nana, if Bogey would choose to talk now, what do you think he would say?"

Nana laughed and said, "I think he doesn't have to talk. His purring says it all."

Bogey's whiskers twitched and his paws moved a little as if he was running. His little mouth was open a tiny bit and I heard a slight snore. I knew he was sound asleep and dreaming.

I leaned over and whispered in his ear, "I hope you're dreamin' what I'm dreamin' cause I'm planning our next big adventure."

Why cats purr is unknown. It is believed cats purr when being loved, petted, or are relaxed. Some cats purr when they eat!

Months Later

Napping on my pillows used to be my favorite thing to do. Then Mattie turned my life upside down. Now I love to wake up to the noise of those cowboy boots running down the cottage path.

I pretend I'm asleep when she stomps across the porch. She scoops me up in her arms and shouts, "BOGEY! I'm back!" I act surprised every time. I know what's coming next, the big kiss right between my eyes. Mattie laughs when my eyes cross.

She visits most weekends. We spend the day talking to our animal friends, exploring the forest and having picnics by the pond. Mattie still looks for fairies in the trees.

❧

A cool breeze blew across the marsh and tickled my whiskers. I wrapped my tail around my body and cuddled close to Mattie. I rested my head on her tee shirt, the new one with my picture on it. I'm not as comfortable here as I am on my wicker sofa, but Mattie loves the rope hammock.

We could hear the ocean crashing up on shore, if we were quiet, which was almost impossible with Mattie around.

"Next time I come to visit, I'm going to bring Tucker," said Mattie.

"Are you going to bring Gus and Buddy too? So I can see a goldfish and a hamster?"

"No. The last time they rode in a car, Gus jumped out of his fishbowl. I thought we'd never find him under the back seat. And Buddy got car sick. I'm never gonna do THAT again! But I'll bring Tucker! He loves to ride in the car."

"I hope he likes me. I don't want to spend the whole day scrambling up trees," I said.

"He's gotten over chasing cats. Trust me. He'll like you. The two of you have never been to the beach. We're going to. . . ."

The screen door banged.

"Mattie... Bogey... where are you? Supper's ready!"

"We're coming, Nana," yelled Mattie. She whispered to me, "Let's do it the usual way. On the count of three. One... two... three... Go!" Mattie yelled.

We fell through the air and I landed on top of Mattie's stomach. I rolled off and flipped on my back. We giggled.

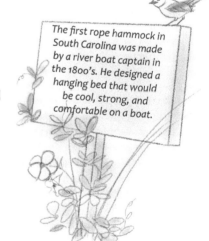

The first rope hammock in South Carolina was made by a river boat captain in the 1800's. He designed a hanging bed that would be cool, strong, and comfortable on a boat.

"I've always liked to watch the bottom of this hammock swing back and forth, haven't you, Mattie?" I said.

"Bogey, you're so silly. You say that every time we fall out of this hammock."

"I know. Wanna race to the porch?" I asked.

"Sure, but you have four legs, Bogey. I've only got two. You always call me a slow poke, so give me a head start," Mattie insisted.

"No way," I said.

"Okay then, GO!" Mattie called out.

We raced hard and fast. My four legs carried me ahead. I was almost to the porch when I heard a big plop.

I turned around. Mattie lay on the ground. She'd taken a short cut and tried to leap over the boxwood hedge. Her red boots stuck out of the top of the hedge.

"Mattie! Mattie!" I said as I rushed over to her.

"Oh, oh. Oooooooo," She moaned. Her eyes were shut tight.

I put a paw on her shoulder and bumped my head against her face. Her eyes flew open.

"JUST KIDDING!" she screamed and jumped up.

It took me a second to get my legs moving. She'd done this to me before. I fall for it every time.

Mattie giggled and raced past me. I couldn't help but smile as those red cowboy boots clomped across the porch and blond curls flew around her face. She dashed through the door and yelled over her shoulder, "Comin' slow poke?"

The King of the Plantation
An Ode to Bogey

When visiting Bogey, there's two things he asks,
That's plenty of meals and affection.
If you can't find the cat food, there's no need to fear.
For he'll willingly give you direction.
A tap from his head on the white pantry door
Means "Open it up, I need FOOD!!"
If you're slow to comply, a small nip on your leg,
To remind you, he's not being rude.
When he sits on your lap he's a happy old chap
And won't move a muscle for hours,
But start shifting around and he'll turn with a frown
"You're waking me up," and he glowers.
He has a sweet habit of hugging his rabbit,
Whilst licking its ears and its face.
It is only a toy, but it gives him great joy.
To throw it all over the place!
He's a cat with a story, he lives now in glory,
Enjoying a safe happy life.
But his young days were tough, he had to live rough,
And survive through much trouble and strife.
When you meet him you'll see, and have to agree,
That this black and white laddie IS fat.
But at the plantation, they pour a libation,
To BOGEY, that King of a cat!!

–Julie Whittaker
British visitor and admirer of Bogey

About the Author

Jean Hunt's inspiration for this book began when she and her husband bought a home that was once part of an old plantation on the coast of South Carolina. Wildlife and animals live on the land that is surrounded by huge oak trees, marshes and woodlands and is the setting for the story. Out of the woods strolled the cat they named Bogey. He brought with him a raccoon and a squirrel. The three adventurous animals settled into a peaceful routine in their new home. Jean based her story on these amusing characters and her love for nature and animals.

About the Illustrator

Caroline Lott and Jean Hunt's friendship began when Caroline painted a portrait of Bogey. Caroline listened to Jean's stories about her special cat and an idea was born for Cat Tails & Spooky Trails. Majoring in commercial art, Caroline studied under internationally recognized illustrator and portrait artist, Brian Jekel and later earned her Master's degree in fine art. Originally from Southern California, Caroline now lives in South Carolina with her husband and her dog, Mac.

About Bogey

Bogey is a stray cat that one day discovered he liked people. Shy at first and after much thought, he decided to be friendly to Jean and her husband. They had moved into a cottage near the woods where Bogey lived. His timing for love, friendship and nurturing could not have been more perfect. Everyday the Hunts drove to a Charleston hospital for cancer treatments. Somehow Bogey sensed he could help and took his job very seriously. He waited patiently on the porch for their return each afternoon. Bogey insisted Jean and her husband relax and enjoy the marsh wildlife and introduced them to his funny woodland friends. The rest became a beautiful story of love, friendship and devotion between a cat and his adopted family. Bogey now spends his time greeting guests that come to visit his family's cottage. They all leave with a sense that they have met an amazing cat named Bogey.